DARIA'S ALIENS

DEDICATION

BOOK - MA

This book is intended for mature audiences for adult language, sexual content, and violence. It deals with parental death, polyamorous relationships, emergency healthcare, sex with multiple partners, and other adult topics.

VÒLLⱯIAN GLOSSARY

ĜHA – PERSON WHO MAKES MY SECOND HEART BEAT, SOULMATE.

PEHOLOE—ELDERS WHO HAVE LOST THEIR GHA

VÒLLØ – ONE OF THE MAJOR ALIEN RACES ON SHOJO, USED IN THE SAME WAY WE USE HUMAN.

JISA—THE ANATOMICAL SHIELD THAT PROTECTS THE SKIN. THE VÒLLØ HAVE IT NATURALLY, SOULMATES DEVELOP IT THROUGH THEIR BOND.

B'ATU—ANATOMICAL BUMPS ON A MALE VOLLO'S PUBIS MEANT FOR STIMULATION.

ĻÀĻÈ – SWEETHEART

B'IJÀCHINĔ – SOMEONE WHO HAS MULTIPLE MATES GIVEN BY BASO SHEVA

VÈTSØ – A CURSE WORD LIKE DUMBASS.

D'O GO CHU MERCHU—MY ENERGY IS YOURS

ŘŮŞAD'Ù – A TRADITIONAL BONDING CEREMONY ON SHOJO

HØ—A DIMINUTIVE FOR CHILD

PRONUNCIATION GUIDE

RIHU- REE-WHO

ROYI - ROY-EE

WUPESO- WOO-PAY-SO

VALKARRA - VAL-CAR-UH

VÒLLØ - VAH-LOW

ĜHA - SAID LIKE A PLEASING SIGH 'AHH'

ĜHAJO - AHD-JAY

ŘŮṢAD'Ù - RRR-SAW-DO

B'IJÀCHINĚ - BEE-JAW-CHEE-NAY

YISO
VALKARRA
WUPESO

Chapter One
Daria

I wanted to go home. The aliens were nice, and Demi seemed to adjust to Wupeso well, but I missed my dad, coffee, and my romantic partners. I missed being able to sit at my table after work and hear about Malik's day, crash on my couch with a pizza while Anthony picked a show for us, or meet Nasha for a workout in the gym. I even missed the nights we all slept in the same bed, even though I hated how hot it would get. But the thing I missed most was a sense of normal.

On this planet, it felt like I could never find normal. As soon as I got used to one thing, a new creature popped up, or an illness, or some new religious lore.

On Earth, I had normal. I was a busy person. As a nurse at the hospital, I worked long hours. Then, I spent my weekends driving the two hours to visit my family with whichever of my partners could spare the time and emotional tax it was to see my mother sick. I was active in my community, and I had three romantic relationships to attend to. It always turned out okay because Anthony would cook dinner for us, and Nasha would step in to help Malik when he needed it, and they all loved my sister Demi as much as they loved me, so they didn't mind sleeping on a twin bed in my childhood home so I could be there for her as my mom dealt with cancer. I was busy, but I had a support system full of people I loved. Life was a bit sad but normal.

Then, my mom died. And she bought Demi and me those tickets to space and told us to "touch the stars." Now, I'd crash-landed among those stars with a pod full of strangers, Lightyears away, and I wanted to go home.

Today had been another long day, hiking across Wupeso to check on the pregnant women and making six-month checkups with Blossom to gather more data on how the humans were adjusting. Then, I had to track down Demi after her warrior training and make sure she ate before her evening plans with the new Novak girl. Then, Rihu and Royi found me and just wanted to flirt, even though all I wanted was to find Buttercup and talk more about the rocket science I needed to learn to get the hell off this planet.

Now, Demi's dainty breaths collapsed against her pillow across the room as I stared down at the tablet Blossom gave me to borrow. I was looking at complex diagrams of the escape pod and its engineering, trying to make heads or tails of it. The blue light from my screen was especially unnatural on this planet, and looking at it for too long always gave me a headache. Months without daily-use technology had made reading complicated schematics in the dark harder than before.

I've read everything there is about the escape pod, from hull integrity to maintenance guides, and all I knew for sure was I needed a space mechanic or I needed to become one. I needed someone who could understand the intricate power and navigation systems and comprehend how they work, then fix them in a way where I could make it back to the SS Herculean, use the hyperdrive technology there, and return to Earth. According to Blossom and Buttercup, this was a statistical improbability. According to me, staying on a planet with cave monsters and magical mating bonds was a statistical impossibility. But my goal required me to know all the things, so I read and studied the pod.

In the scheme of things, there was only one thing I didn't need to know: Blossom promised me she had synthetic intelligence integration covered. She also promised that my attempted research would improve my chances of returning to Earth to two-point-nine percent rather than the less than one percent it had been six months ago, but we were still here. So, how much could we truly trust her calculations?

SS Herculean Escape Pod 3, Main Ship Integration. Subsection B, Manual Ejection.

I had read the section three times, and my eyes were blurring. With a sigh, I set the tablet beside the glow lamp on my bedside table and closed the wood mechanism. I wouldn't be getting anywhere if I couldn't learn from the information I was scouring. Still, sleep evaded.

Outside the *peholoe* loft—a sprawling building located atop a karst beside beautiful, lush floating islands—the dull roar of rushing water and deadened sounds of wildlife floated in. Truly, the loft should be called the human loft since we outnumbered the elders who lived here two-to-one. Over the past months, sleeping here took adjustment. I was used to the sounds of city cars zooming by or spending my nights inside a hospital emergency room triage. Inside the loft, it was quiet, aside from the few snores of the humans still living here. When Priscille brought back a second escape pod filled with humans and her own alien pirate boyfriend, it felt a little crowded. Perhaps less lonely as well.

Sometimes, I'd hear people panic or scream. I wasn't the only one plagued with nightmares from the *SS Herculean*. Who wouldn't be? The chitinous beasts with thousands of eyes tore through human flesh as if they were butter, squeezing human beings into a red, meaty sauce like grapes in a press. Despite the luck of us survivors escaping on the few available pods and landing on a friendly planet, nightmares weren't unusual. If you had one, no one said a thing in the daylight.

Some nights, Demi would start to whine and twitch. She would call out for our mother. Soothing only when I laid a hand on her shoulder or snuggled in beside her. Before

Roxie moved to Valkarra, the other alien island near us, I would hear the mechanical slide of her gun as she counted her bullets. So many of my fellow survivors were plagued by the disappointing routine.

Most nights, I could hear at least one girl from *EP 2,* though their nightmares certainly contained more than just ugly, animalistic aliens ravaging people in front of them. They were stuck in their pod for months, surviving on raw alien fish. Buttercup, their escape pod's synthetic intelligence, was less soothing than Blossom from the stories I heard.

Truthfully, the more I learned about the people I crashed with and the other pod members, the more I realized we all had our fair share of horrors before and after the *SS Herculean.*

Unfortunately, it meant even when I tried; I struggled to get to sleep. It seemed like the moment I closed my eyes, they opened again to the soft shove of Demi's hand.

"Breakfast time, D. I have to practice my language arts before I get to the training grounds, and Zhalisee has already been by this morning."

"What time is it?" I grumble, trying to gauge by the light invading through the slatted wood.

"Second hour. We're already on the second sliver of the sun," she explains, giving both the human and *V`òllø* metric for time on this planet. When she's convinced I'm getting out of bed, she bounces across the room to tie her hair into a bun. "And tonight is girls' night!"

Ah, yes. Girls' night. Demi's favorite night of the month and the first true girls' night since the members of *EP2* and Priscille's ship arrived. While they were adjusting, girls' nights were two different affairs. The sea-faring girls had one, and the originals had one. Now that everyone had adjusted (the best they could), Vera, Queen of the Village, determined we needed to have one where every female survivor came together.

It was also my favorite night because it was the one night in the entire month, or moon cycle, where no boys were allowed. Early in the day, the men who were vying for human attention would prepare meals and gifts, drop them off at the *peholoe* loft with the beautiful (but terrifying) Hoga, and then leave us alone for the rest of the night. Kano and the human men would entertain the younger children for the night. Then, the *peholoe* loft full of families and old *V`òllø* would turn into Club Blossom, where all of us women could throw it back and mingle.

It was the one night of the month when Vera, Cerridwen, and Priscille, the mated human women, would ditch their alien dicks, and rejoin the rest of us who were just trying to make do.

I liked it for multiple reasons. One, it put all my patients in one place. So, if Cerridwen's labor stopped being a figment of her imagination, we would already be together. Two, I didn't have to procure a meal for myself or Demi. Before Vera agreed to bone down with Kano, it had been nonstop meals prepared and provided. After? It was like on Earth. We would grocery swap and cook together. Three, and finally, it meant I knew where Demi was.

Keeping track of my teen sister had me aging faster and longing for my parents. Most nights, Demi would stay at the training grounds competing with the *Vòllø* boys her age, or I would find her off exploring the island without someone to make sure she didn't die. Sometimes, she walked back without me, and sometimes, she was impossible to locate. When I would get upset, she would always remind me I wasn't her mother, and finding that balance with her was another challenge I still hadn't mastered. On Shojo, I didn't know how to *just* be her sister without worrying about her safety.

Dragging myself out of bed, I pull myself together, sliding into my linen pants and cropped shirt, while Demi dabs on a bit of the makeup we've invented from the various plants. *Put women on an unfamiliar planet and watch them thrive.* I swear.

"Do you want me to pick you up at the training field for girls' night?" I ask, hoping she won't give me an attitude.

"No. I think I'm going to walk back with Sadie. Supposedly, she will be there today." Demi had been trying to convince the shier *EP2* girl to join warrior training with her. Since the *EP2* community integration has been slow, Sadie hasn't yet managed to show up despite Demi's constant invitations.

"But if she's not there, you'll wait?"

Demi turns to face me with a hand on her hip. She's obviously annoyed with me, but I remind myself that is what it means to be thirteen. And Demi has been through more than a normal thirteen-year-old should. In just the last year, she lost her mother, had her heart broken by her first love, and ended up stranded on an alien planet. Of course, she would want some independence; she earned it. In Demi's mind, this was her revival, and it made me feel completely alone in my desire to go home.

As if my sister can see how much I need the win, she grumbles, "Sure."

My heart sinks in my chest.

Chapter Two
Rihu

There is nothing like the feeling of the drop. When a mount steps off the ledge, and freefall begins. That swooping feeling in my stomach, the staticky sparks along my *jisa,* the way my mind quiets as it realizes control is futile. I live for that feeling, and being a sky warrior feeds it. Though, since recently, it hasn't been the only thing. There is a certain human woman whose presence feels like flying.

"Kano says to do a perimeter check, sweep the islands, and return for training exercises," Royi says, flying up beside me on his mount's back. He was foolish to tame his mount after pipping, but I had to admit his mount's discipline was better than my own.

"Do you want crystal-side or plant-side?" I ask, knowing we will meet at the cove.

"You take the crystals–"

I don't wait for him to finish his sentence because it would have been, 'Meet at the cove.' Instead, I click my tongue, guiding Karo to the left. We were already behind this morning because I woke up late and because I was hoping to glimpse the women on my way to the clearing. The sun was already up, blaring down on the city, and the men were up and moving. Daylight and my opportunities to glimpse a certain human woman were passing. No need to waste it.

As I flew over the crystal fields, I could see Kano and the new pirate fellow walking up to the prayer mats together. Tall spires of fiery red crystal were bound in delicate twists of icy crystalline flowers, bathing the entire scene in a lavender glow. Directing my mount higher into the sky, I scan the karst for dangers—finding the only one to be Hoga, the most terrifying *peholoe,* on her way into town. Passing by the rocky hills, over the southern floating islands, around the colorful rows of farmland, and circling the cove measures before Royi meets me.

Even with my goal of catching sight of a beautiful human today, I don't mind waiting. The cove is exceptional in the morning light. I love how the water sparkles under the sunlight and the way the birds and bugs begin to fly and chirp. I like to see the village wake up or watch Llazho drag in his nets. As grouchy as he is, there's nothing quite like watching him revel in his catch. I don't mind waiting because it gives me time to think about the things I may not have time for otherwise.

Royi, my chosen partner, is a big thinker. He thinks too often and about too many things. Sometimes it makes him feel a little sick from how much he thinks. He also argues that I don't think nearly enough. That I fly by unawares far too often. I maintain that I simply don't have the time to think more, especially for a mess of ugly thoughts.

His arrival at the cove is proof. I didn't get to think a single thing aside from how beautiful my world is and what kind of thinker I might be.

"You cleared the islands? The Valkarrans found more of those sky monsters. We must be prepared for them to find Wupeso."

I slash my tail with mild irritation.

"Of course, I cleared the islands. All is well, *tsaĝha*." It means chosen mate, and it's an assurance Royi often needs.

I can hear his shuttering breath. He nods, and then he dives toward the training grounds, calling, "Last one there cleans the roost."

Chapter Three
Royi

I will clean the roost, even though Rihu's head was stuck in the clouds above the cove, and I beat him to the training grounds without issue. He would not do it the way I liked, and that would only cause me more work than doing it myself. But I still enjoy the look of defeat on his face.

The training grounds are already teeming with life. The Vukusugo, our land warriors, warm up their muscles, while Niore leads the youth through their mind exercises. Each day, the warriors come together to train as the Wupeson military, and each day, this has become increasingly important thanks to the newest threats and our human population. Our military was happy to have women and children to protect again after the death of Baso Sheva.

As beautiful as our human survivors were, they were not physically strong. Their skin was thin; they had no *jisa* to protect them from the elements, let alone a threat, and they slept for far too many hours comparatively. They had been through harrowing experiences, and it showed. When the humans first arrived, many of them acted like prey. They would flinch from food offerings or back away from a tangle. Humans needed protection, especially from the threats that seemed to follow them here.

Tying off my mount, Lari, to a post, I dismount with ease and find my way to the place where Niore works with the children. We have a few Vòllø children left, all of which are male, and they have been training much longer than humans. However, the human children have impressed me with their dedication. The young twins, Cain and Abel, are fast learners, much like the other boys, and they have quickly grown strong enough to spar. Then there was Demi.

She was the human Daria's young sister and a force of nature. She did not allow the boys to tease her or push her around, and she worked twice as hard as them, even if it did not immediately translate to her being faster or stronger. Over time, it often made her better. She liked to work hard and didn't appreciate it when one of the older warriors would invite her to sit out or give her an easier task. If they did, she would begin her *down with the patriarchy* discussion, reminding them that women are capable, and if they claim to revere them, they will give her the proper training. She is much like a traditional *V`òllø* woman in that way.

Today, Demi stands next to a girl slightly younger than her. This new girl arrived with the pirate's ship and has taken no interest in warrior activities thus far. I would have expected her younger and bolder sister to join if the little babe was of a warring age, but not this one. A pleasant surprise.

Demi smiles at my arrival, dragging her new friend forward.

"Royi! This is Sadie Novak. She's finally ready to try warrior training."

I stared down at the young girl and tried a tentative smile. The poor thing shakes where she stands, and I stop. So many of the children barely reach my knee, and Sadie is quite small like them. Demi doesn't seem to notice as she introduces me.

"This is Royi. He's the best at training because he breaks it all down step-by-step. His look-a-like is over there," she points to Rihu, who hazes Niore, "He's pretty good too, but can get frustrated when you mess up too many times."

"Hi," the young girl says, moving her hand slightly at her side. I know this is a human custom, a greeting, but she is so timid that I worry about her reaction if I were to move my hand in her direction. I tilted my horns instead.

"Hello, warrior Sadie."

Her cheeks do that human thing where they turn pink, and I mentally work through how I can make the small girl more comfortable. Coming to my knees, the same way I did when I first greeted the human children, I try a shallow smile again, keeping my fangs mostly behind my lips. Demi keeps an arm around the girl, and I believe it's keeping her from shaking or running off. Then, I offer a hand, palm up. This was something Demi taught me.

"High five," I command.

Her eyes widen slightly, but then her tiny hand slaps into my own, and she smiles. Looking up at Demi, the burgeoning warrior girl smiles and nods in encouragement.

"I told you he was the best."

"Okay, I think I'm ready," Sadie agrees, meeting my eyes for the first time.

I hope she's not disappointed when I sit her down and teach her to tap into her mind.

Chapter Four
Daria

You would think since Blossom and Buttercup were synthetic intelligences and *sisters,* they would know how to get along. Hate to have firsthand knowledge that this is so far from the truth. They bicker worse than even Demi and I, and they seem to hate each other. Instead, they act as a constant reminder that things could be worse between my sister and me.

At first, Blossom was relieved to see one of her sisters alive. She was distraught when she heard about *EP1*, and her sister who ran that ship. But when Buttercup got off the ship, touched Blossom once, and gave a sardonic, "Glad you're not dead," things changed. The beautiful green bot was not nearly as devoted to the human population as her sister, only stepping in when a need was obvious, and her behavior left Blossom wrung out and exhausted. Blossom's patience waned with her within days and now the two sisters spent most of their time apart.

Except for today, they couldn't because it was another testing day. Blossom put out a blanket statement when we all arrived on this planet that we would need regular testing to ensure our bodies handled the refuge planet well and to track any changes that may affect us. It was both a collection of scientific data and a healthcare initiative for her. Somehow, she had convinced Buttercup to help. Even though the green bot had a terrible bedside manner, she had all the same tools and interest in the data.

So, I ignored their bickering as we made our way to Vera's. Our fearless leader stayed the furthest from the *peholoe* loft, out by my favorite spot in Wupeso—a tiny hot spring surrounded by tall purple flowers that smelled incredible. I liked it for the relaxation the natural hot pool brought but also because over half the women seemed to have an allergy to the tall, stalky plant, which meant it was often unoccupied.

As we approach, I wish I could ignore these responsibilities and soak in the hot pool. Or even work on fixing the pod while I soak. Unfortunately, I stand in Vera's kitchen instead.

The houses in Wupeso are interesting, tiny circular homes with walls cutting through the space in a series of semi-circular rooms and hallways. It meant that the first room of a house was often a big open space where the people would cook, eat, and relax. Then, you would wind through your bathing room and closets before finding the bedroom at the back of the house, which held the second most importance according to their culture.

After I take Vera's vitals, Blossom pokes the soft skin on Vera's hand with her needle. After learning that the *jisa* was thinnest there last time, we tested everyone. A minuscule tube of blood, smaller than anything we ever took at the hospital, hides within Blossom's body as she runs a bunch of tests.

"I swear the needle gets easier every time," Vera murmurs, taking a bite of her breakfast. She's not even dressed for the day yet, sitting in only a robe while her foot rubs over her pet's scaled back in soothing strokes.

Magnus is her terrifying pet. Like a monstrous dragon without wings, he snarls at anyone he perceives as a threat to Vera. The first time Blossom drew her blood after Vera found Magnus, the beast nearly took Blossom's arm off. Now, he was well-trained and more docile than a golden retriever pup, just because Vera told him to be. Another oddity that made me long for home.

The mechanical whirring sound happening inside Blossom fills the room, and then she's spouting the changes.

"The effect of the *jisa* on your blood has strengthened. You're taking significantly less sun damage, and your body is running optimally."

"Fantastic," Vera mumbles through another bite of her food. "And no babies?"

"Not yet," Blossom confirms, as if she didn't know Vera's stance on that.

One patient down. The rest to go.

Priscille is my last stop of the day, and I already know she is the most complicated. While the rest of the women all get tested every three months, my pregnant ones seem to undergo constant monitoring. We had to test for staph and gestational diabetes. We would listen for heartbeats and monitor their little half-alien fetus. Cerridwen was always in ultra-panic mode, and I had to remind her to breathe more often than I should. Priscille, however, was so relaxed I wondered if she was partaking in some kind of recreational drug, but her bloodwork always came back clear.

"Daria!" she greets, wrapping her arms around me tight. I hug her back, reveling in the small spot of comfort before she tugs us into her house.

The frontmost area is full of exotic baubles and specialty decorations her pirate husband came with, and she had a proper door leading down a hall to a more human-style corridor with their living arrangements.

Mekho, Priscille's *ĝha*, appears from the back corridor as we step inside, and Priscille takes a seat on a cushion surrounded by books. Holding out her arm for Blossom, I place Buttercup's blood pressure cuff on the opposite side and wait for the symphony of buzzing to begin. Mekho sits on her other side, just behind her, keeping vigil. I'm confident that if a single thing were to go wrong, if a single hair on Priscille's head was harmed, the man behind her would go ape shit.

Soon enough, we have her stats, and she's healthy as a horse like she's been her entire happy pregnancy.

"Any symptoms we should know about?" I ask, preparing myself for the dissertation.

Priscille nods, pulling a book from the center of the stack to her right and flipping it open. It must not be the right one because she looks through two more before she finds the one she's looking for. Flipping it to a page that she's dated according to the days in our current moon cycle, she lists all the little things that have changed with her body.

She notes places of tenderness, that her nausea in the morning has been fading, and that her energy is much improved. She also notes a weird reaction to some wood dust, which Blossom assures her is fine from her blood work, and asks about a dozen questions about the status of her baby.

"Now, according to my calculations, we are near thirteen weeks and could know the sex of the baby," she says finally, closing her book and opening another. She dips a quill in ink and stares at me impatiently.

I look at Blossom, and she begins the ultrasound. With Cerridwen, she was already well into her second trimester before she asked about the sex of the baby, so we didn't have to worry about if it was too soon. With Priscille, this was a guesstimation. She knew when they first slept together; she knew approximately how time converted on this planet, and...

"Congratulations. You're having a baby girl," Blossom announces, showing the ultrasound image as a projection on the floor.

Priscille smiles brightly, tears shining in her eyes as she looks at Mekho. His mouth drops open in shock. His voice is rough when he whispers, "A girl? Truly?"

"You're going to be a girl-dad," I confirm. Priscille doesn't wait for Blossom to wipe the goo from her belly. She throws herself into Mekho's waiting arms. Their lips crash together, and a groan pulls itself from her *ĝha*. Despite the synthetic sisters' desire to ask a ton of questions, I take that as our cue to leave, dragging the two bickering bots out the door.

When we're a safe distance away, and I've sent the bots ahead, I let the homesickness take over and feel the tears begin. Everyone is settling here. They're moving into houses, and falling in love, and having babies, and I can't because I'm still wrapped up in my life on Earth.

Chapter Five
Rihu

Royi had already cleaned the roost and left by the time I arrived. Everything is exactly how he likes it, down to the layer of dry grass beneath the nests. Yet, the air feels different. First, I look over the ledge. There's no storm on the horizon, no swirling of the seas. Then I scan the trees above, but there are no new eggs in the nests, no troublesome creature stealing supporting branches from the tangled beds above. It's not until I make it to the workshop that I hear it.

A soft sob echoes around me, and a burn starts in my chest. Whoever is here, they are sad, and that does not sit well with my *jisa*. Creeping toward the sound quietly, I'm filled with disbelief when I see the lovely Daria curled in on herself, leaning against a tree. My selfish desire to see her had hoped to find her in better spirits. Instead, Daria's shoulders shake, and terrifying slivers of liquid sadness drift down her cheeks. *Tears*, Kano called them.

I don't stay quiet as I come through the brush, letting my feet crunch against the undergrowth as I approach. At a particularly loud snap, her head snaps up to mine, and I can see the redness around her eyes. Her sadness matches the ends of her long, spiraling hair. Even now, she is stunning.

"Oh, hey, Rihu," she blurts, immediately hopping up from her spot on the ground. Something inside me aches when I realize she's trying to hide that sadness from me. A smile like a mask covers her face, though her eyes don't clear fully. For the first time in a long time, I'm torn inside. Should I let her keep her sadness from me? She pats down her gorgeous berry-ended curls before shoving her hands to her sides. I tilt my head, and she must sense my skepticism.

17

"I was just taking a little break," she explains, breathing in deeply through her nose. The watery film in her eyes fades, and I step forward. I don't want to embarrass her, but a deep tug in my chest calls me closer. She needs me like Royi does. She needs someone to lighten her mood.

"I'm great at little breaks. You should invite me next time," I say, feeling myself drift even closer. When I'm around her, I feel more like myself. Daria is like living divinity. If she would let me, I would worship the warm planes of her body and take away whatever pains she cries over.

She makes a half-laugh, half-snort, and her eyes roll in their sockets.

"You always have a line," she mutters, brushing the debris off her pants.

"I understand the translation of these words, but I cannot understand the meaning," I explain, tilting my head in confusion. A line of what kind?

"Like a pickup line. A way to reel a girl into liking you."

"You're not a fish. We're not in the sea. Why would my words reel you in?"

"So you could catch me." She pauses, twiddling her fingers in front of her. A moment of silence passes between us as I imagine her words, but before I can show her I understand, she shrugs. "You're right. It's a weird concept. Forget I said anything. I've got to get to girls' night."

"Wait." I'm not sure why I want her to wait, but just being near her is making me happier. Her presence is soothing after a long day.

"What's up, Rihu?"

"The sky," I reply immediately before a grin spreads over my face. "I see! This is the pickup line. You are humorous, and that attracts a *ĝha*."

She smiles, and her eyes roll again. She shakes her head, making the pink tones of her hair twirl and bounce. I'm mesmerized by it. I think I've misunderstood her again, but she does not explain further. Instead, a faraway look enters her eyes.

"If that was all, I really have to go. Girls' night is a big deal around here."

I still don't want her to leave. My body tenses at the thought, but I nod in agreement. The human women needed their time together. I respected that despite the urge to follow her there. Picking up a tool from the workbench she had been crying beside, I say, "Try the dark pink fruit. That's from Royi and me."

She smiles and leaves me staring after her.

Chapter Six
Daria

"Still want to go back to Earth?" Vera asks, sidling up beside me near my post along the wall. I don't understand how she gets the audacity to even ask me that. Of course, I still want to go home. Nothing has changed for me. Sure, she and Roxie and Priscille have all settled in hard, but I'm still on my own for the first time in years, navigating alien pregnancies and raising my sister. I still go to sleep thinking about how grieved my partners on Earth might be and wake up wishing I had them with me. So, yeah, I want to go home.

"If I said yes?" I respond instead of confirming. Vera is like a dog with a bone with the happiness of the women. When we landed, she was the bravest, the only one able to string together a coherent sentence, and this made her a good leader. Then, she married the acting ruler of the area, and her role cemented itself. She was 'in charge' in a way that made her believe she needed everyone to be happy.

"Really?" The surprise in her tone makes my teeth ache. "But Demi is making friends, and you're one of the most important pillars of the community. I thought maybe…"

"Maybe I forgot about my grieving father? The three other people who loved me most on Earth? My job and community?"

My chest heaves with the weight of it all, and Vera looks appropriately cowed for a split second. Shaking her head, her face goes blank. It's a superpower, the way she hides everything. Half the time, no one knew if she loved Kano. Unless you caught her staring with heart eyes, you could never tell.

The tinny bass coming from Blossom's speakers and the chatter of women on the dance floor seemed so out of place from this onerous conversation, but Vera continued anyway.

"Daria, listen." It's a plea, and I harden myself against whatever she plans to say. Words will never make my losses easier. "You need to settle in here. Blossom and Buttercup are worried about how much work you're doing to fix the pod and that even if you did, it would be high risk to return to the *SS Herculean*. You may never even make it back to Earth. Maybe it's time to cut your losses."

None of this is news. From all the calculations I've run, from everything I've learned, the percentage of return has stayed the same. Blossom and Buttercup tell me every morning, *'Your chances are still less than one percent.'*

"Vera, please. You know nothing about loss. The only person who ever mattered in your life is standing right over there."

Maybe it was harsh, but it was true. Vera is quiet. Her face gives nothing away as we both look toward her best friend. Aston dances with Demi and Sadie. Both girls look at her like she's some kind of popstar. Aston swings around her wild red curls to Blossom's club remixes, and the girls follow her lead. When I pull my eyes from them, I watch a single tear drip down Vera's face, and a tiny stab of guilt pinches in my chest. She looks over at me with a tight smile.

"My sister was getting out of rehab this year, or she got out of rehab probably about three Earth months ago. I was supposed to pick her up. She was going to live with me. And you know, Aston left behind all her brothers. I invited her on the stupid ship because we were going to be space babes together for a time and then go home—where she could still be Aston Andrews, heiress to the Andrews fortune, and artist, and gallerist. Her parents and her brothers loved her dearly. They're probably pouring their millions into a rescue mission for her.

"And Alba's husband died on that ship. And all these *EP2* people who just joined us have experienced loss. Half the children on that pod don't even know what happened to their parents. Poor Lily cries the minute Sam turns a corner.

"But the difference between me, and them, and you is that we are moving on while you cling to a less than one percent chance. We moved forward and focused on what we could control rather than training to become rocket scientists in our spare time, using valuable energy and resources for a long shot.

"And I respect you a lot, Daria. For what you've done for the village and what you are trying to do for yourself, but don't assume you know things you don't."

Vera pats my shoulder before fixing a smile on her face and joining my sister on the dance floor. Pushing off the wall, I leave my full plate on the low table before sneaking out the bathhouse door and to the forest floor.

My mom always taught me that my anger wasn't productive, that it would get me into trouble, but as I stomped through the forests of the floating island, I remembered my mom was dead. I wanted to feel my anger; I wanted to fuel it. But that wasn't who I was and the last thing my mother would want was to see me acting like someone I wasn't.

"You're so level-headed, D. It's one of the many reasons I love you." Malik kisses me on the head.

"I loved your level-headedness first," Anthony mutters, tugging me into his embrace.

A rough laugh escapes me, echoing through the trees. If only they could see me now, storming away from the loft like a petulant child. I stop in my tracks. Despite my dad's inability to get out of bed, I handled my mom's death. I dated Anthony and pulled him into my existing relationships, even though he compared my relationship to that psycho-religious guy with the harem of minors. Even at the hospital, when things got crazy, I always kept my head. Yet, some random girl I've known for less than a year hints at the idea that I should move on, and I *run?* That's not who I am.

Stopping in my tracks, I take a deep breath, grounding myself in my surroundings. Somehow, I made my way to the *uhichi* nests, and Lari ruffled her wings above me. Somehow, I always found my way here when my emotions flew out of control. I smiled up at the mount, trying to find Karo beside her. The two of them were ride-or-die like their owners, so I figured she had to be close by.

A hot breath brushed my shoulder, and I spun to face the massive beast behind me. Karo's chest contracts with her breath, and I reach out a gentle hand. She nuzzles into it, pressing her ridged beak into my fingers. I'm about to murmur about how good of a girl she is when her owner emerges from the shadows.

"Have you been following me?"

Chapter Seven
Rihu

Twice in one night, Daria appeared so unexpectedly. I love the way her eyes narrow on me, the tiny sparkle glinting in them like a blade. The way she reacted when I teased her... Daria is the loveliest woman I've ever met. Still, I'm surprised she's out here. It was girls' night in the *peholoe* loft, and it was getting dark.

"No, I'm not following you. I," She pauses, and my lips curl upward. *She was looking for me.* A warm feeling spreads across my chest. Her brows pinch together.

"It's okay if you were," I offer, looking back at Karo. I can see from the rapid contractions of her chest that she's tired. We took a loop of the entire island, doing Royi's part since he cleaned the roost for us. But I figured if I gave her some feed, she would be ready for another flight. Daria was the only human who enjoyed them as thoroughly as us sky warriors. And I was grateful for our shared interest. "Karo just needs a snack, and then I could take you for a ride."

Her chin dips slightly, and her curls obscure her face. A nervous giggle bubbles forth, and my smile grows. She rolls her shoulders back, and when her eyes meet mine, the beautiful brown circles immediately dart away as if she didn't expect me to be looking at her.

"I didn't come out for a," She pauses to think again. She and Royi would get along, always overthinking. "Vera said some things, and I needed a break."

"Vera says a lot of things I need a break from," I assure her, leading Karo to a bucket of feed. She's a magnificent animal—a sharp hunter, smart in a pinch, well-trained. She doesn't hesitate to eat, recognizing that I haven't unharnessed her. Even with Karo's ravenous munching, I don't miss the humorous huff of breath from Daria. It sends me down mental paths I can't traverse safely.

"Did you know she left a sister behind?"

"Kano said as much." I want to say more, but I don't want to spook her. It's the first time Daria's spoken to me about anything serious. The way she asks makes me wonder if these *things* Vera said forced her to think about being here without Demi. Vera's concern for her sister sometimes consumes her, and she takes it out on the women here by fixing problems and caretaking. Does Daria consider that? She hums in acknowledgment.

"I don't want to go back to girls' night, but I'm not sure I should be out here."

My smile is constant when I'm around her. So, my face doesn't change when I promise, "You're safe with me."

Her eye circles make a loop, but her lips tilt up slightly. I glance at my beast for only a second to check if she's finished, searching for Daria in the dark once again.

"Karo is almost finished. Offer stands."

Daria looks at the sky. It's not quite dark yet, and we can still hear the laughter from girls' night filling the trees. I can tell she's considering it, that maybe she wants to, but something is holding her back.

"We can go fast. Just how you like."

"I don't know. I just left Demi back there. Probably shouldn't."

"But you want to?"

She sighs, and her coils shake with her head. I want to wrap my hand around them, but she has been clear. Touching her hair is off-limits. Daria says she doesn't have time to detangle it. She stares at the edge longingly. *Does she not understand that her longing is unnecessary? We will go there.*

"I love flying. I do. It's one of the few things about being here that I'm going to miss."

I can feel the skin around my horns tighten slightly, and I narrow my eyes in her direction. I hate it when she speaks of leaving as if she does not light up the entirety of Wupeso with her presence. Daria helps the people of Wupeso the most of all the humans. She is a skilled healer, appreciates our culture, and I... well, I feel like a better person when she is around. She sees me for who I really am. I force myself to soften; she misses Earth.

"Might as well take as many flights as you can then," I surmise, calling Karo closer. Early in the days of the new women, Royi and I took the women flying often—aside from Az-ton, who hates the heights, and Vera, who only ever rides with Kano. Yet Daria was the only one who really loved it. She befriended the mounts, would spend time on the cliff side before and after the scheduled flights, and sometimes would even seek me or Royi out for a flight after a long day. Our shared flights were the only time I ever truly saw her off her feet.

As I attach the extra set of loops to Karo's harness, I look over at Daria. She glances toward the loft one more time before nodding in agreement.

"You're right. I should enjoy it while I can." Her tone is not convincing, but when she pulls a smooth fabric wrap from her pocket and begins tucking her curls inside, I know she's committed.

Together, we walk to the landing ledge, and I help her into the harness loops. When they're snug around the thickest part of her thighs, I climb into the loops right behind her.

There is nothing different about this flight than any of our others, but it feels different. My heart beats wildly in my chest, reminding me I am still without a *ĝha*, that this is nothing but a flirty flight between friends. My second heart doesn't beat, and maybe it should for the man I've been close to forever, or maybe it never will.

Yet, her skin is cool against my own, and she relaxes against me with a pleasant hum. Her hands hold onto my thighs, and the gentle dip of her fingers makes my *jisa* crinkle. My mind wanders to other scenarios where her fingers might dig into my skin like that. I turn my mind back to our flight.

With a low whistle, Karo dives from the ledge, sending her wings out wide. She catches a gust of wind that tilts us away from the island. I give her a secret whistle command to 'Enjoy the winds' so she can lead this little adventure safely. I want to focus on my riding companion.

Daria is a vision. She takes in the landscape, and I wonder what it looks like through her eyes. To me, the choppy seas, the floating islands, and the fields of crystal are all normal. But Daria makes me feel the magnificence of it. It makes me wonder what her home was like. Do her people have important crystals like the ones below us? Her admiration of the battle between icy and fiery crystals is clear in her widened eyes. The soft part of her lips when Karo swoops low over the trees of a floating island. The scent of the *hazhiruga* wafts upward on the wind, and I feel her shiver with pleasure. Was there a similar plant where she came from? She laughs with joy when Karo does an intricate pattern of swoops and loops. Then darkness takes the sky for good, and her awe turns toward the stars above.

Daria rests her head against my chest as she searches for the sky. Her face takes on that soft quality it gets when she thinks about the joyful parts of her life before landing here.

It's different from the tension I see when she speaks of her desire to return home. I brush a hand down her arm and whistle low for Karo. Then, as we head back toward the landing, her eyes fall closed, and she murmurs words that are lost in the wind.

Chapter Eight
Daria

"Will you help me fix the escape pod?" I ask the moment we're both dismounted. With the wind all around me and the fresh air invading my lungs, my thoughts had free rein in my mind. Vera's warning words, her urging me to accept my place here, my dread over trying to figure out rocket science, and how alone I feel all circulated in my mind. Then, the stars came out, and Rihu didn't complain when I used him to get a better view. It was like my mom whispered to me I didn't have to be alone. Like she was reminding me that no woman's an island.

Maybe I am the only one who wants to return to Earth, but I could still ask for help—and there were a couple of *Vòllø* men who were happy to help me.

"You want me to help you fix the metal ball you landed in?" If his tone didn't give away his incredulity, the twitch of his jawline and slight tilt of his horn to the left would have. *But he didn't say no.*

"Listen, I've been studying the mechanics of it for weeks and I think I know what it needs. You know tools and power here on this planet, and you're strong enough to use percussive force," I explain, excitement building inside me.

Something about the flight cleared everything up for me; something came over me, and I knew this was the answer. I needed the support that was being offered. He was the answer to everything, and he would get me to where I needed to go.

If I swallowed my pride, I could see my polycule and my dad again. Demi could go home, finish school, and be the most popular girl around because she survived space. I knew if Rihu said yes, it could all happen.

Yet, he wasn't jumping to help like he usually did. He seemed nervous—like he didn't know what to say. He hid his cocky demeanor as he considered my words. Panic and hope dueled inside me. If he said no, the powerlessness would kick back in. I'd have to beg one of the other men, and I didn't trust them with this. If he said yes...

"Please," I beg, taking the heavy leather harness from him and resting it on its hook. Heart thudding in my chest, I waited for an answer. My hand weaves through his, and sharp heat spirals through my veins, urging me forward. I take his other hand and tug on them, waiting for him to meet my eyes. This is the closest I've been to him, but he doesn't seem to mind.

The emerald color of his eyes narrows to tiny pinpricks on me, studying the plea written on my face. If he could sense how close I was to coming apart, he didn't show it. Instead, his lips curled up, his eye color widened, and the sparkle of his *jisa* seemed to buzz beneath my fingertips. It felt like the tickle of wings across my skin.

Inside, I felt like I stood on a cliff side. The wind was the only thing holding me up, keeping me from tumbling off the edge. But if my faith was in its strength, and it changed directions or abandoned me—if Rihu abandoned me—then I would fall right over it. I'd fall to the rocky waters on the bottom, and I might never get back up. Outside, I smiled and squeezed his hands reassuringly.

"Oh, Lovely Daria, you know I'd never say no to you," He teases, twirling me in a circle beneath his arm.

Relief fills my chest, but it's like a painful fire. It spreads from my sternum to my collar bones, dragging a hiss from my teeth. I pull my hands from Rihu's and rub the spot to soothe the ache, but it won't ease. Pulling my shirt away from the skin, I see two perfect sage-colored tattoos lying flat across my clavicle. I know exactly what they mean.

When I look up at Rihu, the grin on his face as he stares at his own chest confirms my greatest fear. My breath becomes shallow, and my smile falls. Rihu peeks down at me, and I can't track the emotions as he cycles through them, but he pulls me to his side, giving me a slight squeeze.

His words are exactly what I need to hear.

"Don't stress, Daria. Nothing has changed. I shall still fix your metal pod."

Chapter Nine
Royi

There was something special in the air tonight. I could feel it. Rihu would be along soon, and in the meantime, I helped his mother, Jaye, set the table on her back porch. Though she wasn't just his mother anymore, I had to admit. She had taken me in after everything and treated me like her own.

For that, I was forever grateful.

Jaye lived among the hills with many of the remaining families. Though she had every right to join the *peholoe*, she wouldn't yet. She swore that Rihu and I were her boys, and she still had family. She didn't need to take up space where she wasn't needed. In return, I made sure the both of us showed up for her. Setting the table was the least I could do.

Our table was close to the ground, surrounded by the tall grass of Jaye's farm. Again, even though she could join the *peholoe*, she refused. She sowed seeds and harvested goods for the town and freely shared her wisdom with Rihu and me. I placed down the stewed greens and flaky fish she'd prepared, scanning the hillside for Rihu.

I don't find my other half, seeing instead all the work to be done in the next moon cycles. Soon enough, storm season would be upon us, and our home was looking worse for wear. Jaye's hard work would need to be harvested and stored. Rihu and I would need to plan for flooding and put an extra coat of oil on the house.

"Royi, *làlè*," Jaye calls, pulling my thoughts back to the moment, "We should eat while it's still warm. Rihu will catch up."

I do one last scan for him before joining her. It wouldn't be the first time Rihu was late for dinner. He got caught up with whatever it was he did without me around, and I worried for him, as per our normal agreements.

I serve Jaye's plate for her. It's a sign of respect for elders, and she insists she doesn't need it. Still, her grateful tangle makes me feel loved, so I do it as often as I can. When she's served, I fold my legs beneath me and serve a plate for myself.

We're halfway through our meal, chatting about our days, when Rihu joins us. He looks handsome, as always. His tail swishes lackadaisically, while his smile is bright as a sunbeam, and there is something different about him. I can't quite place it, but just like in the air, I can feel it. It feels like a shift in the winds, but different. More like a prickle along my *jisa,* a warning.

He swoops into our peaceful dinner with his enthusiasm, tangling horns with his mother and placing a kiss on her forehead. Then, he hops over the table to find a seat by me, knocking his horn against mine like he usually does.

"Someone is chipper," Jaye says, whilst I'm too caught up in my mind, deciphering Rihu's change in demeanor. What could have him this carefree? His pale green hair is windswept around the base of his horns, but he runs a hand through it to smooth it down.

Rihu's smile distracts me, and my eyes stay caught on him as he leans over to serve himself a dish. It's not his words that register for me. His shirt falls away from his chest and marks I would recognize anywhere crackle like his *jisa* on his chest. The realization slams into me before his words.

"I have every right to be. The Baso Sheva has blessed me with a *ĝha.*"

My eyes stick to them; green marks the same color as his eyes, only a shade or two darker than my own. He leans back to eat, and his shirt falls against his chest, hiding them from me. My mind catches up to the moment and the confirmation he gave. He has a *ĝha*.

My fear and jealousy shove down the joy and happiness I want to feel for him. I glance between Jaye and Rihu and see their shared happiness. Jaye's eyes are wide with surprise, her smile the same bright crescent as her son's. She hammers him with question after question, her food forgotten. Meanwhile, my heart feels as though it's collapsing inside my chest.

"What? When? Who is she? One of the new humans, I suppose?"

Rihu's tail flicks at the same time his hand comes to rest on my knee. I jerk at the touch, my eyes snapping to his. *Is that appropriate?* What does his human *ĝha* think about a *tsaĝha?* They are sure to desire the one bond their counterparts have. In a split second, I no longer fit here. Rihu's hand squeezes my knee, and I brush his hand off. I can't make sense of my own emotions, but he doesn't seem to notice.

"Not one of the new humans, but Daria. After my final perimeter check, she was waiting with the wings. We went on a quick flight, and then they appeared." He shrugs.

Actually, *shrugs.* As if Baso Sheva blessing him with the loveliest woman in the bunch is no big deal. My jealousy bubbles up as dozens of memories follow. On her first flight with me, her fingers twined in mine as I helped her from my mount. Our teasing on the beach mere days earlier. How I asked about the pod about her when she first arrived... ...he beautiful healer with the kindest soul. She was the first person outside of Rihu that I desired because she was beautiful, yes. But also for her patient persistence.

Fear comes fast. The idea of losing Rihu's carefree love for me right beside any future I desired with Daria. He would leave me to make a home with her. Then, Jaye would leave me to make a home with the *peholoe*. I'd be alone like I had when Baso Sheva died. No family, no love. I couldn't just tag along like before. My presence would completely overburden poor, perfect Daria.

My appetite flees as the realizations slip further into my heart. My single beating heart keeps me weak and alone.

I stand abruptly. They have been speaking, but they halt. Rihu's tail untangles from mine, and his smile thins slightly. He's probably confused by my outburst, but I don't know what to say. I'm happy for him but scared for myself. I wish Baso Sheva's plans were clearer, but I can't imagine it's for me to stay with him until he leaves me to join her. It can't be that I lose them both in a single eve.

My voice sounds rougher than I would have hoped when I say, "Congratulations. You make a beautiful pair. Excuse me."

Rihu doesn't follow as I make my way to the crystal fields to pray.

Chapter Ten
Daria

The pursuit of pleasure has always caused me problems. First, when I realized monogamy wasn't for me. Then, when I agreed that a space cruise was the perfect way to ignore my grief. Now, with some fated person—singular— that a goddess I don't even believe in has stuck me with. I groan. I just want to go home.

The relief that spread through me when Rihu confirmed he would help me get home soothed the ache of the marks' appearance, but a nudge of discomfort remained. My hope overshadowed my fear as I made my way back to the loft, even as questions collided in my head. *What about Royi? How will he feel about me stealing his one and only?* Then, back to the pod. *I have the manpower. Now, how do I get my hands on the pod? I just pissed Vera off. I'm not sure she'll want to give it to me...*

Demi dances with her friends as I slip past the party and into our room. I try to be inconspicuous, since I couldn't go another round with Vera tonight unscathed. My emotions were still fresh, and I knew I'd have to apologize to her before I could ask for what I needed. Groveling would have to come later.

The marks still burned, like they're not finished lasering themselves into my skin, and to be honest, I'm curious about them. I wonder if they'll ever feel right or if my human body isn't adaptable enough for them. I want to see them, touch them, and study them. *Will I have them after I leave? What biological processes do they affect? Can I survive on Earth with them?* The urge to test them, ask the other mated women dancing outside, is almost enough to have me face people again.

Instead, I ease the beaded doorway out of the way and back into its original position to avoid detection. Then, I find myself in front of the shining surface we use as a mirror. The cropped halter-like top I wore covered my chest well, so I swapped it out for one of the looser swashbuckler-style shirts I used as a nightie. Leaving the top untied, I pulled it open to check out my collarbones.

The look I got in the dark forest through my halter top didn't do them justice. They sparkled under the dim glow of the crystals on my bedside table, bringing with them more questions and fear. My intuition seemed to promise me they were a good thing, but the longer I looked on, the more I tore them apart.

I liked Rihu—I'm sure I was the only woman from our escape pod who did. Most of the other found 'the twins' to be annoying, which didn't change when the other escape pod women showed up. Yet, so much of what I liked about him was wrapped up in how he was with Royi. Royi was his other half. He made Rihu think ahead, and Rihu helped him let go of the things he couldn't control. Their flirting played off the other, and half the time, I wondered if they had a relationship of their own.

They lived in the same home, attached at the hip, and the idea of both of them at the same time was hot enough to burn me to a crisp. Which only heightened the issue of these stupid marks.

I knew from my sixteenth birthday onward that I had more love to give than one person could handle and that I had more needs than one person could meet. Sure, maybe these alien men differed from my human experience, but what if they didn't? I considered the possibility that the appearance of these marks would hurt Rihu or Royi, or both, and that they could hurt me. Not to mention the possibility of pain we would all be facing when I finally escaped this planet and went back to what was good and normal.

Unable to look at them anymore, I tie the strings into a knot. Tightening the sleep shirt, I strip out of my linen pants and find my way down the hall to the bathhouse.

With the promise of help on the pod and a conversation with Vera on the horizon, I wanted to soak away the thoughts swirling around in my head. Since girls' night was such a big hit, and still going on in the main living area, I figured I'd be safe to take a dip without questions. If I wasn't worried about breaking my neck on the karst steps in the dark, I might have ventured to my favored hot pool, but the bathhouse would do.

The room appeared empty when I arrived. Thick steam scented like the purple flowers I loved so much permeated the space, but the only sound was the soft burble of the naturally filtered water. Slipping out of my sleep shirt and into the water, the aches of my body recede.

Being the only human medical professional on the island meant a lot of walking and hiking across Wupeso. Usually, it didn't bother me. Today, after the flight and the new ink, and the hopeful future, the hot water was exactly what I needed. As my muscles relaxed, my eyes fell closed from the pleasure. I felt like I could breathe fully for the first time in days, and it was incredible.

The water shifts, and my head snaps to the far corner of the pool.

"Daria," Hoga greets, dragging me from my moment of peace and capturing my attention. She moves across the pool gracefully, and I wonder when she arrived. Had she been there the whole time? Water drips across her icy skin, and I'm truly surprised to see that it's not freezing against it.

Everyone in the *peholoe* loft knows Hoga is not one to mess with. Her cold features do not affect her demeanor, and her advice always feels frigid. She gives it to you straight. Most of us don't appreciate it as much as we should—except for Vera, who, the more I think about it, the more I realize, must be a sadist.

"Hoga," I reply, giving her a tight smile. I sink lower in the water, covering myself up to my neck and hopefully hiding my marks, but they brighten on my skin, giving me away.

"Baso Sheva has blessed you with a *ĝha*, it seems."

Great. Outstanding. Now, I'm going to get 'the talk.'

"It seems," I grumble, finding a seat along the wall and folding my legs under me. Why couldn't it have been Zhalisee who saw them first? At least she would have answered my scientific questions.

"You are not joyful."

"I want to go home."

"Home is where your second heart beats," she announces, as if 'home is where the heart is' is groundbreaking advice.

"Yes, but on Earth, *my home*, there is a second heart, and a third, and a fourth, all missing me."

Her eyes narrow, and she tilts her horns to the left in obvious disagreement. These marks are sacred to her people, and I'm sure I've just performed the worst form of sacrilege. Yet, while part of me is happy they've appeared because I like Rihu, the rest of me wishes they would disappear. These marks are an inconvenience in more ways than one, and now, they're not a secret inconvenience. If I wanted an *ĝha*, Rihu would be one of my first choices, but only beside Royi.

"You are *b'ijàchině.*"

39

There is no explanation. My earbud won't translate the meaning. Still, it resonates. The label washes over me, and my body seems to say, *that's it*. My body reacts with a hum of approval before I do. The new marks sparking beneath the water.

Hoga tilts her horns to the right, smiling in my direction. She seems pleased I've agreed to her words.

"I'm not actually sure what that means," I explain.

"You have *ĝhajo*. They will appear in time," she explains, standing in her fully nude glory and exiting the water. "Be faithful, and your many hearts will arrive much faster now that your marks are."

"But what if I don't want *ĝhajo*? I don't want *ĝha*—let alone multiple."

The possibility that I could have more than one person here, even by their weird alien standards, soothes some of my questions while simultaneously complicating the most important goal—going home. Still, when I say the words, they don't feel as genuine as that intuitive rush I got when Hoga told me what I was. I glare in her direction, but the *peholoe* gives me a withering look. She says nothing, but I feel reprimanded anyway.

Chapter Eleven
Royi

I didn't go home, sleep beside the person I was closest to, or wait for him to do the morning perimeter check. I slept in the nests, and a gentle rain bathed Shojo in the night. It was a sign from Baso Sheva that things were changing; rain cleansed the land.

Lari didn't like the rain. Neither did I, especially as mud slipped beneath my feet. Mounting Lari, she begrudgingly began our flight. Unfortunately, the fine mist bathing the island made a deep fog across the land. We had to fly low to the ground, and Lari had to hold a glowing crystal in her mouth—which was the one thing she hated most.

With luck, the first sliver of the sun would bake away this mess of moisture. However, the angry clouds above left me little hope—kind of like the silence from Baso Sheva the night before. I prayed for hours; *what shall I do?* No response, not even a wave of comfort. After hours, the nothingness she provided seemed answer enough. I would do nothing except my duty to my village, and that was simply so Kano would not send me away.

Last night, I concluded that being far away from Rihu and Daria was the only experience that could hurt worse than being outside of them. Here, doing my duty to the village, I could keep them safe. Their joy would be on display. I might be outside of it, but at least I could bear witness to it.

My mount banks around the southern karst, diving low along the hills, and my skin prickles. Jaye's home is beneath us, and the itch to land and see Rihu is strong. Still, we move on, ignoring the draw I felt in favor of ensuring the safety of the island and avoiding Rihu instead. Perhaps if I were smart, I could busy myself with extra work to avoid him indefinitely.

As we swoop close to the Helleboralis fungi and the chasm, I can see water cascading down the dark rock and into the yawning pit below. The water is low enough, but if it rises, there is no telling what it will bring with it. If this turn of weather becomes a turn of the season, I would need to keep our eyes on the area. Maybe Kano would allow me to stand vigil overnight.

As we glide through the final pace of our flight, I see Vera's creature, Magnus, still safeguards Kano's home. The fields are free of danger, and the floating island above is soaking up the water. In our quiet village, all is well. Now, if I get to the training grounds early, Rihu may be too busy with his new *ĝha* to notice my absence.

Chapter Twelve
Daria

I wish I had the time to kick Demi's ass. Something about her attitude will always drive me to anger. Even on Earth, it was that way. I could go to work, get fists thrown at me, clean up literal refuse, grimace at my paycheck, show up at home to a dirty house and some petty squabble, and I would keep my cool. Then, I'd drive out to see my family, I'd bring one of my partners along, someone would cut me off in traffic—I'd let it go. All to walk straight into the front door of my parent's home and have Demi look my outfit up and down to say, "Yikes." And that would be it. My cool? Lost.

When we bicker, it escalates. Friendly, cuddly sisters? No, stop touching me. We crash-landed on an alien planet, and we can't even agree on if we should leave.

"I can't believe you won't stay even now that you have a mate," she argues for the fifteenth time. I tug at her hair as I slick it back, and she hisses. She caught sight of my marks this morning and assumed we'd be staying. When I told her the person on the other end of these marks was the one helping us leave, the bickering escalated. Now, as I helped her with her hair, we found ourselves trapped in a cycle of silent treatments and sharp, pointy jabs.

Right now, I was silent.

"You're really not going to tell me anything?" She grumbles again.

Her hair is almost finished, and that's good because we have places to be. She's running behind for warrior training, and I have two pregnant patients who need daily check-ins, and someone is bound to have hurt themselves already, and a talk with Vera is in order—and all of it must be done while dodging my new paramour.

"No," I respond.

"If you can't talk to me about it, who can you talk to?"

I tie off her hair and stomp across the room to my own things. I'd picked an outfit before helping her, but now that Demi saw the marks, it felt too forward-facing.

"Our dad. My partners. Anyone back on Earth when we return."

"Daria, I don't want to leave."

Blowing out a breath, I fist my hands at my sides. *Don't explode. Don't explode. Don't ex—*"So you just want to leave dad alone? You think losing Mom wasn't hard enough But now his daughters too?"

I'm not playing fair. I know that, but Demi is hell-bent on taking the easiest path. She's created an idyllic little bubble here at the expense of our normal lives.

"Don't act like dad is the reason you want to go home! Before Mom started dying, you were hardly ever around. Too busy with your half-dozen lovers."

The dull *thunk* of my heart falling out of my chest hurts. I can't recognize my voice when I spit, "Don't talk about them."

"Or what? You'll drag me back to Earth, deny a supernatural bond, and ruin my chances of being a warrior?" She scoffs. "I think you've already done that."

She walks past me, flipping me the bird on her way by since she can't slam our beaded door in my face. I bury my face in my hands. When I look up again, I see my reflection in the mirror. The marks sparkle on my collarbones like they're trying to cheer me up. With a huff of frustration, I change my entire outfit to cover the marks before stopping in the kitchen for breakfast.

Hoga gives me a knowing look from her place in front of her Neked'I game, glancing at my well-covered chest before moving a chip. I give her a sharp shake of my head before picking up a piece of fruit and dashing out of the *peholoe* loft. She doesn't need to cause me more problems. I have enough of those to last me fifty lifetimes.

As I step outside, I realize the weather reflects how I feel on the inside. There's this thick fog and a heavy feeling in the air. The muddy ground slows my movement. On the inside, I matched. Just as unclear and bogged down. None of my goals were happening swiftly, and there were plenty of obstacles in my way. One of which I planned to tackle this morning. Leaving my arguments with Demi behind, it was time to talk to Vera again.

As I walked through the village, I played it through in my head. I would apologize for making assumptions last night. Then, I would compliment something about her—maybe her beautiful Rapunzel hair or her choice of *Vòllø*-eating pet. *Yeah, that would be good.* After she was sufficiently buttered up, I would ask about the pod.

After my marks appeared in what I'm dubbing *'god's sick joke,'* Rihu mentioned it would be easier to work on the pod if it were near the floating island's landing. For both testing and proximity to his tools, he needed it up there—and away from prying eyes. He also promised the sky warriors mounts could move it if they worked together. It's how they got it near the cliff sides where it sat now, awaiting Vera's renovation skills. With his mind on the logistics of the move, convincing Vera was the final remaining task.

On the main road, only a few people were out. Town was practically empty. I worked my way through the streets, ignoring my usual route to avoid Rihu. Llazho was out, dragging his nets in from the bay. A couple of warriors headed toward the training grounds, but otherwise, it was a quiet morning. The normal bustle of *Vòllø* was dead, like they saw the sky outside and decided it wasn't worth the trouble.

I wished I could do the same, but I still had a goal—get back to Earth. That started with an apology.

Knocking on the side of Vera's door, I wait in the hushed air, nervously looking between her rabid beast that snores beside my feet and the doorway. I hear them moving around in there, but Kano takes his sweet time coming to the door. And, of course, it's Kano that would answer.

"Daria. Are you here to see Vera?"

I want to say—'No, I'm here to see the pope.' But of all the aliens on this planet, he would be the last one to understand.

"Yep. I felt like I owed her an apology for my behavior last night."

Kano turns back to face his living room, and a silent conversation passes between the two of them. I'm unsure of if they're doing the intracranial conversation that the other *ĝhajo* do or if they can just pass notes back and forth via the way they look at each other. They do this for a good three minutes before Kano finally smiles in my direction and motions for me to come inside.

Vera and Kano's home is *homey*. Their main area has cozy cushions on one side and a low kitchen table in the center. One thing I've noticed about Wupeso is that they like to sit when they prepare food. Unless it's outside, then everyone stands until it's time to eat. And they sit close to the ground like Vera is now.

"Good morning, Daria. Kano was just on his way out to check on the sky warriors, so you have perfect timing."

She offers me a cup of alien coffee, but I refuse. It was just another thing that made me long for Earth. Then, I joined her in her mountains of cushions to talk.

Swallowing my pride was a bitter pill, but if it meant getting off this planet and back into my normal, I would do it. In the early days after we arrived, the girls decided Shojo was a good place to exist. They liked how the men fawned over them. They felt grateful that we landed on such a friendly planet. Then, even as Kethi lied to Roxie, and we discovered that the monsters that attacked us in space were present on this planet, and we welcomed an entirely new pod of women, they behaved as if this place was home. In fact, the women of *EP2* only made the situation worse. They were so happy to be out of their escape pod and off of the rough seas that they didn't complain about anything— not even the lack of electricity.

"So, what is it you wanted to talk about?" Vera asks, knowing full well what I said to Kano.

Like ripping off a bandaid, "I wanted to apologize for last night. Making assumptions about you and the other women was wrong. I'm having a hard time adjusting and didn't realize others were too."

"Apology accepted. Now that that's over, and we're talking, I heard a little rumor."

This is it. This is the moment she tells me she knows about Rihu.

"Rumor is Royi didn't go home last night. Rihu was here first thing this morning, asking if we had seen him. Poor Rihu was worried sick."

I feel like the helpless bird in a cartoon. My comical gulp is audible to the audience, but the person I'm speaking with is entirely oblivious to my inner terror. My accidental but

47

systematic dismantling of Rihu's life had already begun without my consent.

I didn't know that Royi didn't go home last night. I knew nothing that happened after Rihu left me on the floating island. It must have been because of me. But Rihu and Royi couldn't fall out. There was no way I would allow that.

I planned to leave, so there was no reason it would be my fault. Yet, my marks felt like a fresh brand beneath my clothes.

"You're close with the both of them," Vera says. "Do you know what happened?"

For a split second, I thought about telling Vera about my marks. Then, my long-term goals creep back into my mind.

"No, but I might be able to find out. Rihu promised to help me with something, but I need to ask you a huge favor."

"I knew the apology didn't come without strings. You drive a hard bargain, but name it." She adjusts her legs beneath her, leaning in slightly.

"The escape pod. I want to move it up to the ledge and try to fix it. If I can, I want to go home with whoever will make the journey."

"To Earth?"

I nod.

"Daria, I'm a gambler, and that's a risk I won't take."

"I'm not asking you to. Roxie, Priscille, you, and some others have made an actual home here. You've found love and now there are babies involved, but my family, my partners, are on Earth."

"You would put your sister through that risk?"

My heart clenches in my chest, and the marks burn once again. Since Demi's outburst this morning, I've been wondering if there was an alternative. Could I leave her here? My dad would never forgive me if I did, but I would have to beg her to go. She would have to touch the stars, just like me.

"Demi knows where she belongs," I explain.

"You really think you can fix it?" Vera's expressionless face hides behind her mug of alien caffeine.

"I've been studying for hours every night, and with Rihu's help, I think I have a chance." I wince internally. Mentioning him after being unable to add to her juicy gossip could have been a tell.

"What is Rihu going to do? These guys don't even understand electricity."

Vera takes another sip from her mug, placing it on the ground beside her.

"He's my muscle, and he knows how the crystals work. My theory hinges on their energy."

"What if you try to, and it doesn't work?"

"Then I'll try again."

My heart beats fast now. Vera is silent as she weighs the pros and cons in her head. She is a self-proclaimed gambler, and she married the veritable king of our little village, so I'm sure she's working through all the plays, counting the cards in her head to see all that she holds. If she wanted to know, she held my future, my hope, and my power all at her fingertips.

"You can try to fix the pod, but in exchange, I want to know everything that's going on between the two sky warriors."

"Done."

"And Daria?"

"Hmm?"

"If it doesn't work, I want you to promise you will try to make a life here—a good six months of effort before you try the pod again."

The risk weighs on my heart, but the excitement overrides it and pushes me forward.

"You've got a deal."

Chapter Thirteen
Rihu

I've searched everywhere for Royi. His outburst is so unlike him that I'm the one concerned. He rarely allowed his emotions to rule him so simply, but I couldn't find another reason he wouldn't have come home.

When he stormed away from dinner, I thought maybe he forgot something in the nests—like the talk of my flight with Daria spurred a memory, and he had to check on something. That's usually what that meant. Then, he never came home. He never crawled into bed with me. I woke in the middle of the night with my *jisa* feeling suffocating and my marks burning, like something was wrong. Only the shock of him not being there kept me from crawling my way to Zhalisee's home for some kind of checkup.

Now, I was trying to determine what had happened. Was it my *ĝha* marks? I wrote that off entirely. We spoke, at length, dozens of times about how happy we would be if either of us were to find a *ĝha*—a true *ĝha* since marks never took for the two of us. Then, I figured I was right in my first thought. Something was obviously wrong with his mount. Yet, when I checked the nests, Karo and Lari were happily nested beside one another with buckets of feed ready for breakfast. It was proof enough that he had already been out to check the perimeter without me.

As unusual as it was for me, I agonized over my words the night before. I simply explained how it happened. He congratulated me.

My confusion chafes, but I know he will be at the training grounds. I'm heading in that direction when Kano catches up to me. His horn knocks against my own.

"Many blessings, Rihu. I have exactly what you need."

"You know where Royi is?"

Kano nods. "He's at warrior training. He has been since before the sun."

"*Do go chu merchu, Baso Sheva.*" Relief spirals through me. I'm glad he is safe, but why didn't he come home?

Kano repeats my holy words, turning me toward the crystal fields.

"Care to tell me what's going on with you two?"

I toss my horns from side to side. Even if I knew what to say, which I didn't, I wouldn't trust Kano with it. Ever since he bonded with Vera, he was as bad a village gossip as the *peholoe*. He used to curse their names for the drama they caused. 'Always between his horns' he would complain. Then, the moment he bonded to his *ĝha*, he wanted to be between everyone else's horns.

"I wish I knew," I offer instead. I want to walk away, but my respect for him keeps me glued to his side. Kano was Rogeshu, after all. It's not like Baso Sheva could die again and make that not so.

"Is there anything else you may want to tell me? Like why a certain human woman was on my doorstep at the first sliver of the sun."

Apparently, this day would be full of surprises.

"Daria went to your home?" This question contained no new information for my Rogeshu. Kano had known about the women Royi and I were interested in since the beginning. While Royi only had eyes for Daria, I was slower to reach that conclusion. It's not that my interest belonged to others, but that the novelty of new women, members of our village, appealed to me. Plus, I had Royi—my perfect partner—already in the wings. The flirting was good fun for both of us.

"Did you not send her?" Kano asks, his brows knotting in confusion.

"She must have gone to ask Vera about the escape pod."

I mention nothing of our new marks. From the look on her face when they appeared, I knew drawing attention to our new status would only push her away further.

Like promising to help her escape the planet, vètsø?

"What does she need the pod for?"

"She wants to return to Earth. She thinks that if I help her fix the pod, she can do so." This was no secret. Yet...

Kano stops in his tracks. We are mere feet from the entry to the crystal fields. Massive spires of fiery and icy crystals grow and jut from the lilac sand. Kano's hand comes to my chest, pulling me to a stop with him.

When my eyes meet his, they widen and narrow slightly.

"But the sunthetic smarts both agree that the chance of survival is too low. When Buttercup arrived, it was one of the first things My Vera asked."

His hand falls from my chest, and I look at the sky with thought.

"Daria assured me that, with my help, the percentage would go up. Something about percussive aid."

Kano shakes his head like the humans do before leading me further into the crystal fields. The morning mist hadn't dissipated, and it did not seem the sun would make an appearance this sun cycle. Frosty air and a foreboding sense that the storming season was on the horizon took root in my bones.

The events of the last several slivers left me feeling completely unlike myself, yet a step onto the sacred grounds of Baso Sheva and a peace unlike anything I've known before comes over me. It felt as if my marks themselves made me closer to Baso Sheva, like I could hear Her words within me. As I knelt beside Kano, who prayed under his breath, I didn't need to say a thing to gain guidance.

Assurances poured into me. My path was clear. Sheva would be with me. Faith was of the utmost importance. The feeling went on and on like this until Kano stood from his spot beside me.

Together, we walked out of the sacred sands. Then, I had two paths to walk. One led to my *ĝha*, where I would likely find good news and a fulfilling project. The other led to Royi, my family, where unexpected discord reigned. I knew exactly where I needed to go.

Chapter Fourteen
Royi

Daria's sister was the first one to join me on the training grounds. She looked worse than usual, but I said nothing. Her face looked pinched, brows pulled together, lips turned downward, and she looked more like her sister in this way. It was another thing I did not mention.

Instead, the two of us sat together and stilled our minds. Demi had improved her mental fortitude much since she first started training, and it showed in her form. Helping her train today would be the perfect distraction.

"Demi, is your friend Sadie returning today?" I ask, tilting my horns to the right when she squeezes her eyes shut. *Something was wrong with our little warrior.*

"Quieter, Royi. Please." She murmurs, gulping down water from her wooden cup. Every warrior had their own, to scoop rainwater from the catch. When the humans came, the Vukusugo demanded that the males carve their own, as was traditional, but a young *Vòllø* boy made Demi's cup. The intricately carved cup was much nicer than any warrior's cup had any right to be. He carved a panoramic view of the island into the side, with a sun stretched along the horizon. Tiny details, like homes and special plants, decorated the sides. Water dripped into the crevasses as she pulled it from the catch, now full to the brim.

"I don't know if Sadie is coming. She barely talks, let alone to me."

The young warrior girl was not herself today. She must have had a lot of fun at girls' night. As I'm about to ask about it, she interrupts.

"Looks like you've got trouble of your own."

I turn to face the direction she points with her tiny hand to see Rihu. He looks tired. I wonder if he slept as poorly as I did. Yet, he walks across the training grounds with purpose and forces me into a tangle. It shocks me. It's comforting.

I jerk my horns from his hold and bare my teeth. His eye color widens.

"You are angry," he says, much like I would if the roles were reversed. For the first time, his tone is empty of mirth.

I am furious. I feel slighted by the Baso Sheva, thrown to the wayside. Worst of all, I felt I could not talk to anyone about it. Kano would wish to play mediator. Daria would blame herself. Jaye would have to choose her true child. I shiver. Sleeping in the nests left me cold to the bone and tired. All I wanted to do was avoid speaking of it, work it off in my training, and return to the nests for another night alone. It does not appear I could be so lucky.

"I'm happy for you, but I do not want to take you away from your obligations," I explain, noticing we've gathered a crowd.

Always oblivious to his surroundings—not a quality feature for a warrior—Rihu does not notice.

"What obligations, Royi? Why are you angry? Something has changed, but I cannot find it on my own. I need you to tell me what it is."

He always does this. Rihu could simply tell me he's confused; he's asking for clarity. But he skirts the meaning of his words, and he needs me to solve his riddles. Inside, I want to. Outside, I explain I can't do that for him. He has to figure out his life on his own now.

"So, you cannot tangle with me. Nor sleep in your bed beside me. Or wake me for the morning perimeter check because of this thing? Is this thing, perhaps the Lovely Daria?" He hisses.

"You are baring your hearts recklessly. Did you consider your *ĝha* may not appreciate that?"

I look beyond Rihu's shoulder at the beauty entering the grounds. I'm so aware of her. Like I have been since she stepped foot on the island. She looks lovely today—as usual. Her curls are bound in cloth, and her dress is modest. She scans the yard, likely for Demi and possibly for Rihu. I don't miss how she lights up when she sees him here. Her light does not dim when her eyes land on me, but I ignore the way my heart leaps.

Our little warrior, Demi, sees her sister and steps from beside me to one step behind. I imagine they had their own spat this morning.

"Great news," Daria states, glancing between us.

I'm sure even a human could notice the differences between us. My shoulders bunch, my horns held high and away from him. His hands are loose at his sides, but his jaw is tight. Or was. When Daria rests a hand on his arm, all the tension drains from him. When she touches a hand on my arm, I nearly jump from my skin.

Whatever her great news is, she does not say.

"What's going on, guys?"

"Royi is angry with me."

My horns tilt. "I am not angry with you. I am simply angry."

"Because Daria's marks appeared for me."

"No." If I argue further, they will know the truth. I am not angry because of that directly, but it would appear that way if I continued. Moreover, my anger stemmed from the injustice of it all. My faith shook, and my singular heart shattered.

 Daria steps back from the both of us. We groan in unison at the loss.

"Twins," Demi whispers to Sadie behind me. I feel less like a warrior for not noticing the young girl's arrival, but I'm too ensconced in Rihu and Daria to greet her.

"This isn't happening," Daria states, looking between us with a firm look.

"I assure you it is," I promise.

"Unassure me, then. Rihu is helping me leave. That was my good news. Vera approved our use of the pod."

The way her eyes flick away from us nervously tells me there is more to the story she is not saying. Rihu is not so observant. I say nothing.

Rihu turns from me to face her, and I turn to escape. Unfortunately, a wall of small girls stands before me, and Daria is not finished twisting her blade.

"Rihu is going to need you when I'm gone, Royi. I don't like that you're fighting."

The news that she would leave him hurts. I ignore it. The two small girls allow me through, trailing after me to train for the day.

"Vera said yes?" I hear Rihu ask.

"Yep. One step closer to gone," Daria murmurs. If my mind were lost like my second heart, I would have sworn I felt Rihu's anguish in my soul.

Chapter Fifteen
Daria

Priscille's house looms ahead, and I'm dreading the appointment. It didn't seem like the pregnant women needed constant monitoring, but the synthetic intelligences overrode me. Luckily, Zhalisee offered to check in on Cerridwen today. So, I only had one patient. Unfortunately, that patient was the most neurotic.

Before my hand can knock on their door, Priscille rips it open with a beaming smile on her face. Just the look of it exhausts me. She doesn't wait for me to enter, coming out instead and closing the door behind her.

"Where were you last night?" She asks, leading me around the side of her place to her decadent little porch.

Her husband, Mekho, has done a beautiful job of creating it. Apparently, all the ship repairs he'd done throughout his life made him a half-decent carpenter, and he was working under the village builder to learn new skills. He made the rocking chair for her and recently finished a crib. Priscille was quite proud of that one. She had been working on her sewing and weaving skills and had since become the place all the girls went for blankets and tailoring.

"So, what symptoms are you experiencing today?" I ask, trying to remain focused.

"Gloomy mood, though I blame the weather. Feeling big, too, though Mekho has been very good at making me feel wanted." She winks at me, and I'm thoroughly scandalized. I take notes on Blossom's data pad. Priscille keeps talking.

"I also have this weird symptom where my doctor—"

"Nurse." I never wanted to be a doctor. As a child, people talked a big game about doctors, but my experience of them was short and clinical. My nurses walked me through clinics, took my vitals, and explained my care plans. They seemed to run the office, and they knew my name. Then, when my mom was first diagnosed with cancer, I was fifteen. The nurses were her biggest champions. The doctor prescribed the medicine, but the nurses gave it to her with all their hope for her recovery on the side. They were the reason I became a nurse myself, and there's not a moment I regret that decision. Even now.

"Understood. So, I have this terrible symptom where my nurse completely ignores my questions."

"What questions?"

"Where were you last night?"

"Priscille, please."

She rests a hand on her belly and another on the arm of her rocking chair before carefully lowering herself into the cushioned seat. With her toes pushing against the ground, she rocks.

"It's just a question, not an inquisition."

"I went on a flight."

"Oh," She hums, "With who?"

The sparkle in her eyes concerns me most. This was one thing I didn't have on Earth—a bunch of snoopy women asking me about my personal life. It's like cable TV and short-form videos on our cellphones didn't survive the pod crash, so what were we left with? The universe's oldest form of entertainment—gossip.

The only way I could see out was through.

"Rihu. And yes, *ĝhajo* marks showed up on both of us. They're green, and they sparkle when I think about him. They did not show up on Royi, too, which is both a negative for the two of them and for me, since I'm pretty sure Royi liked me first. Not that it matters because as soon as I fix the pod, I'm leaving. Feel free to share with anyone and everyone."

The nasty gray clouds seemed to swell with my admissions. The weather felt oppressive. Worse, I could see a look of pity growing on my pregnant friend's face. Then, at the last second, it changed to a more somber look.

"Can you tell me about your life on Earth?"

That question threw me off guard. Priscille wasn't my friend. She was barely my patient. Yet, something inside of me begged me to talk about it.

Part of me needed people to understand why I was so miserable here. On Earth, love had surrounded me. I had a purpose and a future, and my poor father was alone without us. Demi didn't think I cared about him, but I did. There was more than one long night where I wished he was here so that he would at least know we were okay. That we weren't part of the bones and viscera left on the *SS Herculean*. I wanted my dad to know, and my partners.

Meanwhile, my deal with Vera was like an omen at the back of my mind. If I couldn't fix the pod, I'd be forced to make friends. And honestly, it was hard carrying this all alone.

"What do you want to know?"

"What do you want to get back to so badly?"

Good ole Priscille, driving right to the heart of the issue. I considered how the ex-nun might feel about my relationship style on Earth. Then, I remembered she married an honest-to-god pirate, and I let it go.

"My dad. And my boyfriend Malik, and his boyfriend Anthony, and my girlfriend Nasha. I also would have thought Demi wanted to go back to her ex, but apparently, *Vòllø* boys are cuter."

Priscille refuses to acknowledge my attempt to talk about Demi. Or redirect our conversation away from me.

"What are they like?" She asks.

"Malik is outgoing. He always knows how to make it a good time, whether we're staying in or going out or six days into a ten-day road trip and exhausted..."

The memory of us all crammed in Nasha's Jetta, halfway to the coast but still in the middle of nowhere, crashes through my mind. There were cornfields on both sides of us and signs warning that we were liable for the cost of any cows we hit on the road. Anthony was upfront with Nasha, while I cuddled up in the back with Malik, and they were bickering nonstop. Then, Malik, at the top of his lungs, started a game of I Spy—where the only thing he ever spied was corn.

My lips tilt up in a smile.

"And what about Nasha?" Priscille asks, drawing me back into the present moment. So, I wasn't cuddled in the back of a Jetta with blankets stuffed at my feet and a faded Kermit the Frog stuffie in the back window. I sat cross-legged on a hard wooden deck with the crushing sound of a waterfall at my back.

"Nasha was a goddess. I didn't even know I liked women until I saw her. She had these stunning hazel eyes and freckles across her nose and forehead. I noticed these first because she busted her nose and sat in the ER bay during my first rotation there. She had these long, dark twists in her hair and full lips I wanted to kiss, but I had to be professional.

"Long story short, Nasha asked me out, saying she had to explain how she got the broken nose."

I leave out the part where it was from getting in a fistfight with her best friend's wife-beating husband. I knew I loved her then.

"And what about Anthony? You called him Malik's boyfriend, but you said you wanted to get home to him, too."

"I was the one to bring Anthony into our little bubble, but after he joined, he kind of became Malik's person. So even though we all love each other, I guess it's an inside joke. Anthony is Malik's boyfriend. We all come after in his eyes."

"That doesn't bother you?"

Used to questions of this kind, I shake my head. Love wasn't a limited commodity that had to be claimed and hoarded. It was an open field of energy that multiplied the more you used it. It's not like I stopped loving family just because I found a boyfriend. I guess I never understood why another partner was any different.

I loved Malik; he loved me. We both had more love than we knew what to do with, so Nasha joined. And then, I fell in love with Anthony because he was so different from the sunshiny optimists I had in Malik and Nasha. He could see the dark parts of me and not turn away or try to fix it. That worked for me and Malik, and eventually, he won over Nasha, too. All the love just kind of culminated between us, creating something special that my heart ached to have again.

"Do you think that could happen here?" Priscille asks, "That you could have more than one *ĝha* out there?"

I scoff, remembering the tension in Rihu and Royi this morning. If they were meant to be in a polycule, they were doing a shit job at showing it. My marks show up for one of them, and immediately, their peanut butter and jelly friendship falls apart like soggy bread. Jealousy was a normal part of polyamory, but their showdown at the training grounds looked like the basis of an irreparable break.

Plus, I wanted to be focused on leaving Shojo, not fixing issues between two full-grown men over petty jealousy. They would know this if they asked me how I felt. But communication between us died when the marks appeared.

Unfortunately, I couldn't negate the idea entirely.

"Hoga said I was something special and that they would start showing up if I did."

Priscille pouts. "You told Hoga before me."

"I think Vera knows too."

Her brows crinkle.

"Don't stress. It's not good for the baby," I told her, resting my hand on her knee.

I watch her pull in a deep breath, then an 'oof' follows. Her face twists into a smile, and I think I know what's happening. Before I can ask, she tugs my hand to her belly, and the tiny foot of a baby presses into my hand. It feels miraculous that this life was even a possibility, but to have proof of it beneath my hand—the odds were looking good on the miracle front. So, maybe I would make it off this island.

Chapter Sixteen
Rihu

"You really think you can fix this?" Kano asks, slapping a hand against the metal exterior of the pod. The sound seems to reverberate across the island, spooking the birds. My *jisa* felt tight over my skin from the labor.

Moving the pod was no easy feat, but the worst was still ahead.

"I'm going to have to," I explain, looking at the complicated drawings Daria provided me. "Baso Sheva gave me the marks *after* I accepted Daria's proposal. If I don't prove that I'm an honest man, I have no chance of her staying."

My slight familiarity with the pod doesn't help as I locate the latch for reopening the door. According to the drawings, much of the maintenance access is inside the metal hunk. They did this because repairing it in space, which Blossom has described to be perilous, would be the most likely scenario.

I find the latch, and the door opens with a hiss. Everything about the technological ship was fantastical. From its shiny exterior to the mechanical components that we could only hope to recreate one day, the pod was a work of art. One I would have to master if I were to win my *ĝha*'s heart.

Stepping into the pod, Kano follows behind me. I was a fixer. Solutions came naturally to me, and that's why I was never as worried as others were. I trusted everything would work out for me. Fixing this pod, and winning my ĝha would be no different.

"So, how are you going to do it?" Kano asks, looking around the musty space.

Vera had kept it closed since they moved it toward the cliff side. Since it blocked part of their view, the pod annoyed

Kano, but Vera insisted it was a friendly reminder to get started on the project. Before approving Daria's use of it, Vera planned to refurbish it into something she called a *'doghouse'* for her pet, Magnus. Blossom left it in *low-power mode*, whatever that means, and there was now a thin layer of dust across the surfaces. It smelled odd like there was a complete lack of Sheva in its creation.

Lights flickered on as I stepped into the center of the room, bathing the space with its unnaturally yellow hue.

"According to these drawings, there is a false door over here," I say, pushing a small circular indent between two bed areas. Another pop-and-hiss noise happens, making Kano step back. Then, the false door opens to reveal tons of ropes and strings of various colors. "This is where I will work if I intend to modify the pod to fly to the stars."

With his arms crossed over his chest, Kano wraps his tail around his leg. He doesn't look happy to be inside the vessel that brought him Vera, but I am. It was my turn to win a *ĝha* from this blessed beast.

"This makes me uneasy. Surely, the human Daria should stay. This pod can make My Vera's special pet home."

"You worry too much, Kano."

"You worry too little."

Maybe he's right.

I drag my hand across a rope that is wrapped in something blue. At first, I'm surprised; the texture is unnaturally smooth but tacky against my hands. It feels like the plant we used to make glue, but the color is too bright, and it leaves behind no residue. My surprise turns to wonder when I reach toward the top. Before the blue covering disappears into darkness, it's been cut off, baring twists of metallic strings. I compare what I see to the drawings I have below me and try to make sense of the various markings beside them.

I turn to face Kano, removing my hands from the odd panel pieces. It's extremely unfamiliar, and I probably need Daria's help. Maybe Blossom's, too. Yet, none of that causes me concern or worry. Learning, especially to help my *ĝha*, is a noble cause. The mistakes I make along the way will only aid me.

"You are a faithful man, Rogeshu. I'm sure you can pray a little for my success."

Kano's brows narrow on me, and I only smile back. His tail flicks against the ground.

"I will pray you grow up, Rihu."

"Never," I promise.

Chapter Seventeen
Daria

Three days after my fight with Demi, she speaks to me for the first time.

"I'm staying late at warrior training tonight."

She has freshly washed and styled her hair, and she's dressed in her practice armor. She doesn't look at me when she speaks, but she's obviously waiting for a response as she looks at her reflection.

"Okay, great. Do you have a new friend or?"

She's silent for a moment, and I wonder if the seven words I heard were wishful thinking. The last thing I need is for this tantrum to go on longer than it already has. Last night, I asked her what she wanted for dinner. She completely ignored me, ate a piece of fruit, and disappeared into our room, all in front of the other women. Aston said, and I quote, "Damn. Icy, much? I'm grateful I don't have any teen sisters." Staring at the side of her head, waiting for an answer, I'm about to give up. Then she finally answers me.

"Royi is giving me extra training. I asked him to."

Gratitude for Royi washed through me, and for the umpteenth time, I wish my marks would show up on him while simultaneously hoping not to tie him to me. Royi was a stable presence in Demi's life, and he has been since we arrived. Demi wanted to learn to be a warrior, and while some of the other men seemed uncomfortable with the idea, Royi embraced her wholeheartedly. Any day I worked, he was teaching her something new. He helped her find her limits and master her mind. Honestly, he helped me with those things.

"Do you want me to walk home with you? Since it will be after dark?"

"No."

I wring my hands in front of me. She wasn't happy about our impending departure, but at least she was talking to me. I wanted to keep it that way.

"Are we good, Demi?"

"We good," she says, her warm eyes flashing to mine. My hands go still. Relief remains out of reach.

"Good."

"Good."

We don't speak another word as we finish getting ready. The sound of our shuffling fills our room and nothing else. The clatter of beads pulls my attention to the door as Demi says, "Well, I'm off. Peace."

I'm left staring after her.

Making up with my sister was a good omen—I thought. As in, previously. Now, I know better. Anything involving my teen sister is cursed from the get-go. As proven by the labor I support the moment I walk into my first patient's home.

Cerridwen walks up and down her living room rug as her contractions come at regular intervals. I can tell when they come by the way she squeezes Zhu's hand until his *jisa* crackles. They're about five minutes apart now. She's halted in place as she rides it out, and I watch the stopwatch on Blossom's data pad.

When I arrived to hear her groaning with pain, I didn't wait for Zhu to open the door. It was clear from the puddle on the floor that her water broke, and she was officially in labor. I immediately sent Zhu for Blossom and Zhalisee, and he returned in record time.

Now, the entire crew was here, and the sun was gone from the sky. Village healer, synthetic intelligences, and ER nurse are all gathered together, watching as Cerridwen waddles back and forth unhappily. She has been in active labor since this morning, and she glares at Zhu as if this is all his fault. He doesn't seem to mind. Instead, he rubs a gentle hand between her shoulders, offering a wan smile.

"Get this baby out of me," she growls, her own protective *jisa* sparking along her skin.

"Do you feel the urge to push, Cerridwen?" I ask, drawing her attention from the alien that she looks ready to murder.

"No urge. Just pain. Ah!" She squeezes Zhu's hand tighter. His jaw twitches. I watched the stopwatch. Her contractions were getting longer and closer together. It passes, and she paces the rug again.

We've already determined how she will position herself when the time comes, and now we're waiting to work with her body's timing.

Looking around the room, I realize that we're as ready as we're going to be. Stacks of extra linens are folded beside me, Blossom is monitoring her vitals with a kit no one knew she had, and Zhalisee hums a traditional birthing song that seems soothing and sonorous. Zhu does his best to be a good birthing partner by pulling in enough oxygen for both of them and reminding her to breathe. So far, things have gone smoothly, but I knock against the wood-panel floor for luck. We are ninety minutes past when she dilated fully; she needs to push soon. The length of this labor was making me nervous.

Another contraction hits, and she gasps.

"Okay. Now, now I'm ready."

Together we maneuvered her into a comfortable squat with Zhu supporting her from behind. Zhalisee and I share a look before we urge together, "Push."

Cerridwen works hard. Sweat beads on her forehead, and her teeth clenched so hard I think they might crack. Yet, it was only the beginning. We celebrate her effort, urging her to rest and telling her when to push. Another hour passes, and then finally, the baby begins crowning.

"You're doing good, mama. Home stretch."

Cerridwen focuses on breathing and pushing, and more time passes as her child makes its slow descent. Tears track down her face, but Zhu is there to brush them away. I don't know what he whispers in her ear, but it seems to help because she pushes with renewed vigor. With Cerridwen's cry, loud enough to wake the village, her baby finally joins the world.

Zhalisee catches the tiny tike in her arms. We wait on bated breath for the screech of a baby, but the little thing doesn't cry. I wipe the goo from the nose and mouth, and then we get a tiny screech. Relief drains the color of Zhalisee's eyes, and she slides the crying babe into Cerridwen's waiting arms. There's mild relief, but we're not out of the woods yet.

The sound of chirping outside penetrates the fog of our shared focus, and Cerridwen finally smiles. We help her into a more comfortable position as she clings to the plum-skinned child. I defer to Zhalisee for some alien equivalent of an APGAR score because not only am I not an OB nurse, but everything I know was meant for a one-hundred percent human baby.

With his crying and a quick reflex test, she's confident that he is completely healthy. Tiny horns pop from the thick patch of copper hair on his head, and his little lips are a few shades lighter than his plum-colored skin. Other than the vibrant skin color and the horns, he looks fairly human—like a perfect combination of his mom and dad.

After a few minutes, the baby falls asleep on Cerridwen's chest, and we help her deliver the placenta. The birth was longer than I would have hoped, but Blossom assures me her vitals are stable and urges us to give the new family a few moments.

Zhalisee moves to the kitchen to mix up an herbal tea that will help with milk production, and Blossom promises to stay close by. I step outside and stretch my legs. The sun rises on the horizon, burning away the leftover mist from the day before and filling the sky with fluffy white clouds, so similar to the ones on Earth.

My legs and back ached from all the kneeling and squatting and bending we did in the hours and hours of Cerridwen's labor. But the sunshine does its job and begins melting it all away. With my face toward the light, I breathe in the fresh morning air. Reaching my hands beneath my mane of curls, I lift them from my neck, allowing the crisp breeze to cool the sweat from my skin.

I'm ten steps away from the house when Zhalisee calls for me with panic in her voice, and a chill sweeps down my body.

"She's bleeding too much," the healer explains as we jog toward the house. "I went to deliver her tea, and Zhu was holding the *hø*, and she said she was feeling faint and nauseous. There is a pool of blood."

"Fuck," I mutter, moving to a full run. Snatching fresh linens from the stack as I enter the room, I see Cerridwen for the first time. I hand the linens to Zhalisee to deal with the blood and massage along Cerridwen's low abdomen, cursing myself for not trusting my intuition. I knew something was wrong before, but here we were.

"How are you doing, mama?" I ask Cerridwen. Her eyes bounce back and forth between the healer and me.

"Not good," she slurs.

"Her blood pressure is critically low," Blossom announces, making Zhu's eyes widen. I know this is serious because Cerridwen doesn't immediately become panicked at the announcement.

"Are you loaded up with Pitocin?" I ask Blossom, continuing to massage Cerridwen and hoping it will help.

"My available medications only include pain-relief measures and anesthesia."

Fuck. That's just great. Super fantastic. Cerridwen whimpers as I press upward on her low belly. Zhalisee and I exchanged meaningful looks. We have to do something. Cerridwen needs an unnatural amount of oxytocin and some pain relief to let it through, and she needs it fast.

I stop my massage.

"The Helleboralis," I stand from my place beside Cerridwen and begin rummaging through my medical kit. Zhalisee prepared one for me when she realized how helpful I could be in healing. She set it up exactly like hers, with tiny jars of herbs and salves settled on one side, held on with a net, and tools on the other side. Right near the top corner, a bottle of blue, sparkly, full-to-the-brim mushroom juice sat.

Rushing across the room with it in hand, I pull the stopper from the bottle.

"Drink this." I held the bottle to Cerridwen's lips. The look Zhalisee gives me is reprimanding. We know it can have an adverse effect on our human bodies because it has an abnormal effect on our bloodstream, but all of Blossom's tests confirm it should be fine if the human has a *jisa,* even if it's not fully developed. I also know it works like human ecstasy. We learned that when Roxie was high off of it with her mate sickness. It will help with pain and likely boost her oxytocin levels beyond normal. We watch as the blue liquid empties into Cerridwen's mouth.

I resume my massage.

It doesn't take long after that. Her blood pressure stabilizes, she becomes more alert, and the bleeding wanes.

"Water," I order, watching Zhalisee scramble to retrieve some.

"Cerridwen," I pause, making sure she's present. Her eyes look more focused, but she wouldn't fully recover for days or weeks, and now she would need near-constant monitoring.

"Am I okay? Is my baby okay?"

"You're much better," I confirm. "Baby is fine."

"Her vitals stabilized," Blossom announces.

I direct Zhu to move her to their bed, and with the help of Zhalisee and Blossom, we work out a new monitoring schedule to make sure the bleeding doesn't begin again. The stress of the past few hours hasn't kicked in for me yet, but I know the moment I walk out the door, I'm going to crash.

I just helped a mother of a half-human, half-alien child through prolonged labor, fixed her complication with alien mushrooms, and devised a care plan that included serious infection prevention measures. But I haven't had a sip of water in twelve hours or eaten or slept in almost twenty-four.

Cerridwen's door opens, and we all turn toward it. Buttercup stands there in her green glory.

"I will monitor the postpartum human while Blossom recharges," she states without fanfare. Her mechanical limbs carry her into the room and she stands against the wall as the family recovers together.

"Are you heading to the *peholoe* loft?" Zhalisee asks, and my eyes flick to her like I have another choice. The thought of the karst's steps sends a preemptive burn through my legs, but I nod, even as I stand still by the front door.

"You headed home?"

She nods. "I'll see you tomorrow afternoon. That was good work, Daria."

A small smile tilts my lips. Despite the exhaustion, there was something truly miraculous about bringing the first *Vòllø*-human child into existence. Pride for the experience, maybe? "Thanks. You too."

She opens the door, and I follow her out, closing it behind me. The sun is just a little higher in the sky, and where it filled me with energy earlier, it seems to beat down on me now.

Cutting my way across the main thoroughfare, I use the wooden steps to the beach to shorten my trip. I'm feet from Priscille's backyard when I catch sight of Royi flying above.

Where Rihu and Royi look extremely similar, their mounts could not be more different. The tones of their black feathers shine differently in the sun, the metal latches on their harnesses are different shades, and most noticeably,

Royi's mount has a white beak on the bottom. I wave at them and whistle a hello before looking back to the first set of steps I need to tackle.

I've got one foot on the bottom step when I feel the flutter of wings behind me.

"Are you on your way to the island?" Royi asks.

It's the first time I've seen him alone since I saw the fight he was having with Rihu, and it makes my heart ache. There's clear exhaustion. From the way his *jisa* knits together tighter to the way his chest collapses forward. Even the color in his eyes looks washed out. To see him alone like this makes me feel terrible.

"Yeah." My voice is a little slow, but I explain, "Cerridwen had her baby. A healthy baby boy."

"The entire village has heard," Royi states. He's so matter-of-fact.

There's something behind his eyes, and his horns tilt right. I watch as he dismounts, wondering what he's thinking when he swings me into his arms. My body hums, so my protest is slightly delayed.

"Whoa. Hey!"

"If you're going to the island, I will fly you. You are exhausted."

He's not wrong, so I say nothing as he straps me into his extra loops. Dexterous sage hands brush my thighs to check my security, and I bite back my instant reaction. Like, *down girl. You just saw what these little half- Vòllø babies look like.* My cheeks heat.

Climbing up behind me, Royi's arms come around my sides. He checks the security of my straps one more time, and then a soft click and whistle sends us into the air.

Taking off from the ground is not nearly as smooth or comfortable as taking off from the ledge. Since the floating islands are so high above the island, it's more of a gliding situation. I don't understand the physics of it, but when the mounts are on the ground, they have to create power themselves instead of working with nature. Not that Lari minds. The powerful beating of her wings delivers me to the ledge of the island much faster than my tired legs would have. Before I can truly relax enough to enjoy it, we're landed.

Royi dismounts before me, helping me slide from the straps and ensuring I'm steady on the ground.

"Thank you," I whisper, feeling the effects of hours without sleep. Emotions flood me from Royi's tender act of carrying me within sight of the *peholoe* loft. It would have taken me another hour to get into my bed, and by then, I would have snapped at anyone who looked at me the wrong way. I was tired, hungry, and thirsty, and he made a molehill of the mountain I would have had to climb.

"You're not home yet," He explains, holding me close. I want to argue with him that this will only make the situation between him and Rihu worse. I want to tell him it's unnecessary, but he keeps me off my feet as they throb with pain, and I stay quiet. He carries me through the living area, and I'm grateful Demi isn't in our room when he tucks me in. It's too bad I didn't miss the look Hoga gave us.

He leaves me without a word, and I'm half-asleep when the beaded doorway crackles again. He's quiet, but he says, "Water and food. For when you're ready."

His lips press against my forehead, and an actual tear drips down my face. I'm just so tired. It's then that I remember days aren't the same length here. Cerridwen's labor didn't start at seven am and end twenty-four hours later. I showed up at the first sliver of the sun, and we were three slivers into the new day before I left. I fell asleep with a new respect for Cerridwen and her thirty-six hours of labor.

Chapter Eighteen
Royi

One Moon Later

"You're not made up with Rihu yet? Isn't he, like, your bro?" Demi asks, swinging her sword. Her speed and agility have improved over the last moon cycle. I imagine it has something to do with the lack of swords on her home planet.

"Widen your stance," I order, ignoring the young girl's chatter. Demi did this. She would bring up my issues, adult issues, to distract me from her practice. It was her favorite tactic because it yielded the most results.

"You mean like this?" she asks, taking a half step forward, dropping her center of gravity lower, and attacking me viciously.

Unfortunately for her, she had used this tactic so often that it was no longer providing the same results. I divested her of her weapon before tilting my horns in agreement.

"We have not 'made up,' as you say. He is not my brother," I explain. The women call us 'the twins,' but it's an incorrect moniker. Rihu was my family in a chosen way, my only unconditional love in this world. The *ĝha* marks upon this young girl's sister changed that.

You're happy for him, my brain reminds me. There's no reason not to be. But in the same jar where that reminder lives, there is also the memory of her comforting weight in my arms as I carried her home. When I saw her from above, I knew she needed help. I did not take no for an answer.

"Maybe you should," Demi says, taking her sword from my hand. "I forgave Daria for our fight after three days. And *she* did something wrong."

79

I can't imagine Daria doing anything wrong. And Rihu did nothing wrong either—but I would. If I stuck around while Sheva blessed him with Daria's presence, I would feel compelled to covet and lie. He would love her, and I would wish it were me. I loved her first, after all. I loved him first, too. He would ask if I was okay with everything, and I would have to say I was. *Because you are.*

"Again," I grumble, walking through the sword drill again in my mind. Truthfully, from my mount, I used ranged weaponry the most, but all warriors trained for fighting on the ground, and it was Demi's preference.

"No," Demi argues, tossing her weapon into the dirt. "This is getting seriously stupid. You love Rihu? Don't you?"

I consider lying here. Starting my list of sins. I don't.

"Yes."

"And he loves you." Demi's statement brings me pause, but when she flaps her hands around in front of her, I know she wishes for a response.

"I think so."

"Then that's what's important. I love Daria, even if I think she's being an absolute knob-whacker about wanting to leave this planet. Like, newsflash, Earth sucks. But she's still my sister. I don't want to fight with her."

"Wise words, but they do not apply to me."

"Surrrre."

Demi puts her practice sword away and crosses her arms over her chest. Panic sweeps upward into my chest as she prepares to leave. Like the most pitiful of warriors, I'm using this child as a distraction. Like the heartbroken *Vòllø* I am, I do not judge myself too harshly.

"We're not done practicing," I order, using my practice sword to motion for hers.

"You've gotta stop lying to yourself, Royi. It only hurts you, and Rihu, and my sister." Demi emphasizes her words with her hands.

"Pick up your sword."

"No, I'm not running another drill until you sort this shit with Rihu out."

My mind is rushing over the words that she's saying. This word for refuse is bad, and I think maybe I ought to reprimand her for it. Yet, it has nothing to do with her message. She does not want her training to be a distraction for me anymore. Her advice has been wise, even if her disposition is not. I pin her with my eyes.

"This is not your choice to make. You wanted to be trained as a warrior; now *train,*" I growl.

Demi's eyes narrow in my direction. She crosses her arms over her chest and raises an eyebrow in my direction. We glare at one another for a long moment; then she makes this tiny low-pitched sound.

"Hmm."

And she walks away.

I'm so stunned that she would turn her back on me I can't react. She walks off the field, stopping to steal away her young friend Sadie. Then she stops, points the back of her middle finger in my direction, and leaves.

I'm left with nothing but her words and obstinance. She says I am hurting her sister. That I'm hurting Rihu through my actions. I have not touched him since his marks appeared. Every time I look at him, he is fine, smiling even. And her sister said nothing when I carried her home except

81

to mention her gratitude. So, the answer to this failed afternoon was simple.

Demi was wrong.

Chapter Nineteen
Rihu

Sheva has blessed this day. A beautiful sky, sun glinting off the pod, and the lovely Daria soaking up the sun with her marks on display. With storm season right around the corner, I appreciate every day we have like this. Especially the ones I get to share with my *ĝha*.

I've pulled the directed pieces out of the panel, and we have been working on them together for an entire moon. We made no progress on the pieces themselves, according to her special drawings, but I would not care if this took a dozen seasons. I'm happy to enjoy the journey with her by my side.

"Did you transition the gravimetric navigation system diode directions?" she asks, glancing between the drawing and my mess of colorful pieces on the table.

"The golden spire-like pieces?"

"Yes."

"I changed them yesterday, lovely."

She sits up from her lounging position against the workbench and pushes herself upward. I offer her my hand to help, and she takes it with a small smile. Something about her skin against mine, in combination with the way she looked beneath the light, makes me want to place her on my workbench and make her forget her problems.

She dusts herself off before squeezing herself between me and the workbench. My hands itch to tug her hips against me, but I just press her closer to the bench instead, pretending it is to see her work. Her hands move across the pieces carefully, and I wish they would dance along my skin to the same melody.

Daria is so competent. She understands these alien pieces, and the tiny script across her page does not make her pause in wonder. She moves with purpose, glancing at her drawings and comparing them to the panel in front of her.

"Rihu," she turns her head, and we are nose to nose. My smile widens as her eyes flick to my lips.

"Yes, gorgeous?"

When her eyes meet mine again, my breath leaves me. Her eyes are smoky and warm, like the skies during harvest fires. Thick curtains of hair shade her eyes from the light at my back. Her throat bobs as she tilts her head back to look at me.

I wonder what she sees. Is she as enamored with the view of my face as I am with hers? Does she see her future in my eyes?

"I," she starts, stopping on a gasp as my hand comes to the side of her face. Tilting her face just a little further back, I simply want to see the way her full lips move. Her breath stutters and I can feel my *jisa* ripple.

"You?" I prompted, waiting for her words. I didn't mean to interrupt her nectar-sweet voice.

"I," She stops again, her breath brushing over my skin. We are quiet for a moment. Then she whispers, "Kiss me."

It's easy to fulfill a wish I've been begging for. It feels like a force draws me towards her. Her eyes flutter closed, and my lips meet hers. The sound she makes is one I would sacrifice anything to hear again and again. Part-surprise, but mostly pleasure. It vibrates against my lips as I brace my hand on the bench behind her.

Her back bows slightly as she leans into the kiss, nipping at my bottom lip with her teeth. I nip back playfully, enjoying the moment her tongue brushes against mine. The island we stand on could begin falling from the sky, and I would not change a thing from his moment. Perhaps I would not notice. Pressing her chest against mine, she wraps her hands around my sides and tugs me closer. She feels so right against me like the goddess really created her for me.

Our connection strengthens for a moment, and I can feel her pleasure like my own. It invades my bones and grows in my chest, wrapping me in the beauty of her individuality. She drags a growl from my chest, and my hands lift her legs around my hips. Her hot center presses against me, and the urge to take her here is so strong. But I can't.

As her mouth melds against mine, the tiny twinge of concern she feels sours the heat and reflects my own. This is not how we want it to be. It should be special and whole—different. Despite our bond, we are missing pieces.

I break the kiss. Resting the base of my horns against her hornless head, her eyes sear into mine. There is a sheen across them, and I wish to see her thoughts. A single tear drops from the eyes that captivate me so easily, and I brush it away gently with my thumb.

"Tell me what halts your hearts, lovely."

Her brow crinkles slightly, and her coily hair bounces with the shake of her head.

"I don't want to feel this," she murmurs.

"What do you wish not to feel, Daria?"

I could not imagine what she meant. There were simply too many ideas in her unfamiliar mind for me to think them all up. So, instead of fretting, I waited. If only I were patient enough, she would tell me in just a moment.

"This," she waves between us. "I can't be tied here. I can't love you. And poor Royi. I'm just taking you from him with this selfish mark."

Her breath is choppy, making her chest stutter in sync. I can understand her distress. Her mention of Royi makes my hearts ache. Without him in my bed, by my side, I feel like half of who I am. Daria is stunning, without a doubt, the most winsome of the human women. Yet, the absence of Royi's neat hair and stately appearance in my life hurt. Without the weight of him beside me at night, I could not sleep; instead, I would watch the stars crawl across the sky until the sun forced me from my bed.

My *ĝha*'s head drops against my chest, and I take a soothing breath.

My mother missed Royi, too. She appreciated his calming energy in her home. She calls me her *jaḽisi,* after the tiny birds that fly against the wind just to feel it beneath their wings, but Royi was her *d'osi,* after the animals she used to harvest her weeds and route channels in her farm beds for water. Where I could fly from place to place and feel no difference in my joy, Royi could point his horns toward the stars and carry on with whatever task he had at hand. I missed his focused nature. He was my only love aside from my *ĝha*, and the mere thought of my life without him felt execrably wrong.

I come back to my *ĝha*'s words because I understood her meaning. Me without Royi would never keep her here, even if I could convince her this was where she belonged. Connecting my *ĝha* to me meant connecting her to Shojo and Royi, which she just stated she did not want.

"Lovely *ĝha*," I whisper, placing a kiss on her flat forehead. I want to whisper words of assurance, to explain how I feel what she feels, but I cannot allow myself to feel it too deeply. When I lie awake alone, the feelings threaten to stop my second-beating heart. So, I smile and tease, "You love me already?"

Another watery tear drips from her lashes. She smacks her hand against my chest, and my *jisa* strengthens beneath it.

"You're the worst," she groans, resting her head against my chest. I rub slow circles on her back.

"That may be so, but you are the best, and I wish to be better for you."

She tilts her head back once more and presses her lips to mine. The connection of our lips sends her emotion spiraling through me, and I know there is no way I can handle it all on my own. I need Royi back—for both of us.

Chapter Twenty
Daria

"Do you want to go to the baby shower?" I ask for the third time. Something happened this week at warrior training, and Demi has been impossible to deal with since. She refused to talk to me except to let me know where she would be since I freaked out two days ago and followed her around for hours just to prove we could do this thing the hard way.

"Hmm," she mutters, giving me no genuine answer.

She's talked to *other* people. Hoga asked her to pick something up from town, and she agreed easily. When Vera came by to check in on what I knew about Rihu and Royi, Demi was friendly with her. She talked to Sadie nonstop, even though the younger girl didn't give her more than three words back. Just not me, and apparently not Royi either.

During my little meltdown, where I followed her everywhere, she went to warrior training, but when Royi tried to talk to her, she completely ignored him—choosing instead to train with the Vukusugo. Worse, he looked extra dejected when she did, as if it wasn't enough that I was stealing Rihu from him. I felt so bad then that I had to hold on to the fence to stop myself from running into his arms for a hug. It was all my fault he was in such an awful place, anyway.

Just the thought makes me groan. Polyamory was so much easier than monogamy. If I knew these stupid marks would show up on him, too, or if monogamy wasn't the standard in all my known universe, this would be so much easier.

Not that it matters because you're going home. I'm going back to Earth. Back to Malik, and Nasha, and Anthony, and our happy little shared life. I close my eyes and imagine it, but instead of my crammed two-bedroom apartment on Earth, I imagine a hut by the *hazhiruga* with a bed big enough for me to sleep sandwiched between two massive alien men.

I shake the thoughts away, only to be bombarded with new ones. Like how I should make up with my sister.

Without Demi talking to me, I just felt more alone here. Alone with my vicious thoughts.

They don't even remember you. My mind tells me. *They already mourned you at your funeral. No one knows you're here.*

I wasn't planning on anyone knowing I was here. After my kiss, I imagined bringing Rihu or Royi with me, but anxieties flooded my system like a desert rainstorm. It wasn't safe for the other women or the *Vòllø* people to tell the humans on earth about them. They would want to own, plunder, and control. So, I promised myself even if I went back, I wouldn't tell a soul.

My eyes flick to my sister. *Would she? What about your partners? How would they feel about the marks branding you as a bride to an alien?*

Thoughts had become much too loud recently.

"Demi, please." I'm not above begging. We had maintained a truce, but something happened at warrior training and she refuses to talk to me since. She was locking me out— again. I didn't know what to do. "I don't know what to do," I whisper.

"Fix this." She tells me. "Tell me we will stay here, that you'll do your love is love thing with the twins. That you're done trying to rip my life away from me and ruin the lives of those two *Vòllø* men."

The fire in her eyes is so much like our mother's. My father always kept an even head. Even when he was angry, it was more like a silent disposition than real rage or violence. Not that my mother would hurt anyone, but her looks put me in my place. Demi was never so easy. When they fought, it was fire with fire, and everyone got burned.

"Demi, I can't. I have to go home."

"Why?"

"You know why. Our dad. Malik and Anthony and…" *How many times could we have this same conversation?*

"What about Royi? Rihu? Hoga? These women? Me?" Demi puts her hands on her hips, glaring in my direction. It feels like this is the only conversation we ever have anymore.

"I'm fixing the pod, and you're coming home with me."

"No, I'm not. This is my home now."

"Demi, you have to."

My sister sighs deeply.

"This is why I'm not talking to you guys. But yes. I'm going to the baby shower. I made Priscille a flower crown."

"Demi."

"Hmm," she mutters, grabbing a beautiful wooden box from her bed. I placed a hand on her shoulder to stop her from leaving the room.

"Come back to Earth with me."

Her look of disgust made my heart crumble in my chest, but it was a pitiful comparison to her parting shot.

"Daria. You're not my mom."

Someone transformed Priscille's deck into a wonderland. Aside from the festival Kano threw for Vera and their *r̈uṣad'ù*, this is the first proper event that hasn't happened in the *peholoe* loft or some other mass gathering place. Priscille wanted something cozy and personal, and her friend Clara really came through for her. Little strings decorated in crystals were draped from the porch down onto the flattened pad of land beneath it.

Beyond the beautiful strings of décor, a spicy tea bubbles at the center of a line of flame. Mekho and Kano are grilling other various foods at either end of it, chatting quietly about the differences between fatherhood and the responsibilities of Rogeshu. Mekho scoops something off with a flat paddle and stacks it on a plate with three other pancake-looking foods.

Thanks to Demi's outburst, we arrived at different times, and I was late. I needed time to have a little cry. I'm her sister, and I didn't want to be her mom. If her mom, our mom, was still alive, we wouldn't even be here. We would have watched the horrific news on the couch like every other earthling. I staunch my urge to cry once more while Vera calls attention to the porch.

Priscille looks beautiful. She's only about six to eight weeks behind Cerridwen, yet her bump shows much more than Cerridwen's did. That makes her soft, sage-colored wrap dress look incredible, plus she really has the pregnancy glow. Shinier hair, dewy skin, the whole shebang. Regardless of Vera's supermodel looks beside her, she shines.

"Everyone gather around. We've got a game or two, and then we will eat and do gifts."

When the speaking doesn't ebb at Vera's urging, Aston stands up.

"Everyone sit down and shut up. Let's play some games, yeah?"

The space goes quiet as the attention turns to Vera and Priscille and their spot near the house. Vera helps Priscille into her little rocking chair, and all the women gather closer.

"We have three games planned for today's events, but we need teams of two or three players for each. Take a moment now to pick a team. Priscille will be judge and tiebreaker as the mama-to-be."

I look around for Demi, but I see she's already glued herself to the Novaks' sides. As I look around, most of the women have congregated into groups of threes, and as I'm about to find Cerridwen—assuming she would be a straggler—Roxie swoops in and takes her for herself. Unluckily, Vera sees me unclaimed and drags me into a little group with her and Aston.

Yay for me.

"Sweet! We've got Miss Masters in Alien Physiology on our team." Aston turns to face me. "The first game's alien-baby-themed trivia. So you're going to give us the advantage we need."

"She's very competitive when she's not freaking out about crash-landing on an alien planet," Vera explains.

The redhead's brows crinkle as she glares at her friend.

"It's not my fault I like to be a winner, Vee."

"I'm not even a believer, but God help us all."

"I think you mean Baso Sheva," I offer. It's more than a joke, it's an olive branch. It's proof that I can set aside my quest for an afternoon and that I can mesh with the women here. For Vera and for me.

"Are you feeling okay? I know you're the medical professional, but," Aston slaps the back of her hand against my forehead, before pressing her ear to my chest. "No fever, heart sounds normal."

I step back, smacking her hand away with a glare. "I'm fine. What are you even talking about?"

"You made a joke."

"I do that sometimes."

"Not since I've known you." Aston doesn't wait for a response as Vera moves up near Priscille again to get the game started.

We kill it in trivia. Since my random obsession with the sky warriors taught me everything I needed to know about their mounts and the nursing the aliens and humans alike taught me about everyone's bodies, I had the edge Vera and Aston needed to win.

Demi and I were neck-and-neck for the alien baby food-tasting competition because, back on Earth, food was our love language. For me, growing up cooking with my mom turned into regular cooking for my romantic partners and bringing the best dishes to the barbecue, aside from my mom's, of course.

But I've always been a weak charades player, so by the end of the games, Vera and Aston were both visibly frustrated with me. Somehow, I was supposed to guess stork from Aston flapping her arms about and Vera guessing things like, "Birdie! Golf!" Demi was apparently much better at reading between the lines because she and the Novak girls won.

It felt like salt in my wounds.

"We were so close to three for three," Aston whines, sporting the colorful friendship bracelet Priscille made for the winners. She made one for everyone, but ours all had a tiny crystal bead at the center.

"Get some food. You'll feel less crushed," Vera tells her, sending her toward the tables of food and visiting women.

That's how I found myself alone with Vera once again. She wastes no time.

"How are things with the twins?"

Just the question makes my head hurt. I want to tell her they're not twins. In fact, now that I've spent more time with Rihu, I know they're nothing alike. He's optimistic and poetic, while Royi expects the worst. I want to tell her it doesn't matter how things are because I'm still going home. I wish she'd asked me anything else, preferably something that wasn't remotely connected to mate marks or magic lovers or alien society.

"They're fine. We're figuring things out, making progress on the escape pod."

"I just ask because Royi has been withdrawn. Kano was worried about the two of them. Says their relationship may have been more than we knew."

I'm torn between relief and resentment. She knows about what's between them, likely more than I know, since Rihu refused to talk about it. Completely ignoring the problem seemed to be his preference. Meanwhile, Demi was constantly in Royi's orbit, coming home from training with him to give me the stink eye. It makes me want to talk about it with Vera, but more than that, I want it to not matter. I'm not staying here, even if I'm losing my gumption.

"They're grown. They will sort it out once I'm gone."

Vera's sigh was loud enough that I was worried people heard us from across the field where they were all gathered.

"Daria, what if you stayed? Like truly, just think about it for a second and answer the question for yourself. Terrible statistical probability aside, ask yourself what life would look like if you thought about making a permanent home here. You don't have to tell me if you don't want to."

"I—"

"No, that's much too fast. Think about it. I'm going to go try one of those grilled pancake things, and then, if you want to talk about it, you know where to find me."

Vera doesn't wait for my response, turning to leave me hanging back from the group. Looking in, I can see it— what my life would look like if I stayed.

I'd be friends with the mamas and Vera because Kano is the other main sky warrior. Demi would get to be the warrior she so badly wants to be. I would be with both Rihu and Royi, maybe asking Hoga about her special word for me and what it could mean for the three of us.

Then, I think about the place in my heart I hold for the people I'd be leaving on Earth.

I've never felt like I had too many relationships. Not when it expanded from Malik and me to more, and not when Anthony joined either. Not when our family became close with Mom's best friend during her treatments or when Demi brought her first boyfriend home. The whole time, I knew I could juggle them all. I could love them all. Yet, here, I feel like I'm at my limit. Trying to hold on to Malik, and Nasha, and Anthony while something new happens with Rihu thousands of Lightyears away, and my intuition points me toward Royi and all the women here who want to be my friends.

I'd have to let them go. I'd have to mourn my relationships, mourn my father, and hope that he could survive without us. Then, I could see it. Double date flights with Vera and Kano, Rihu and Royi flirting with me even after a long, hard day. I would train up another one of the human women like Zhalisee does with her apprentice. I'd move Demi and me out of the *peholoe* loft, closer to the training grounds and the hot spring, and I'd go back to my hobbies like singing and hunting for unique crystals. Heavens know this planet has plenty of them.

Yes, life here looked good, but was it good enough to sacrifice my life on Earth? I don't know.

Chapter Twenty-One
Royi

Rihu calls my name from behind me. I have been waking earlier and earlier to avoid him during my perimeter checks, but this morning, I could not pull myself from my dreams. In them, I was not on the outskirts of a relationship between the lovely Daria and the only man I've ever loved and trusted. Instead, I was a part of it. A very sexy part of it.

I did not want to face Rihu when his tender partnership was fresh in my mind. I needed to finish my perimeter check and head to training, where Daria's young sister would continue to ignore my questions and train in silence. My body acclimated to my routine of loneliness.

"Royi, wait."

I halt in my place. I do not know what I am thinking. No good can come of this conversation. From the moment I carried Daria home after the human Cerridwen had her youngling to now, I have been covetous of that which Rihu has. Daria is the finest of her people, the most extraordinary and compassionate. She was soft against me as we flew, and I loved the floral scent of her hair. It was wrong for me to feel this way. She was Rihu's *ĝha*—something else I was covetous of. I always imagined marks would show up for us. It's not as if it was new—the trust and bond between us. I loved him almost as much as I longed for her.

"There is nothing you can say to me," I say without turning to face him. I can hear his steps, feel his energy as it comes closer to mine. I'm attuned to him like he's another piece of me, but I wish it were not so.

His hand settles on my shoulder, turning me toward him and yanking me against him. His horns tangle in mine as his arms wrap around me in some combination of a *Vòllø* tangle and a human hug.

"Royi, I miss you."

I have nothing to say. He feels good. Right. Tension releases along my shoulder blades and slithers right out of my coiled tail. I want this. I need this. Yet, guilt feels slimy along my *jisa*. He belongs to Daria, and I am simply in their way.

I force myself to break this amalgamation of affection and step away from Rihu's outstretched arms. He casts his eyes downward. His perfect smile falls from his face, and a painful itch begins in my heart. This downward turn of his mouth is unnatural, damned by Baso Sheva. It is not who my Rihu is.

"Smile," I demand. Why is he even here? Did I not make my own desires clear by staying away from him? I should not be demanding smiles from him or pleading with Sheva that his arms would wrap around me again. I should shove him away, asking him about Daria, ignoring the fears I hold about inevitable and unending loneliness.

His eyes flash to mine, strobing wide for a moment and narrowing on my face. He does not smile.

"Your brazenness is showing," He growls instead.

Rihu is the brazen one. He is the one who is honest with his thoughts, who charges into danger without care. Rihu is the one with the audacity that keeps him from prayer even in the direst of circumstances. I am reserved. It is the only reason I cling to for why Baso Sheva must have chosen him for Daria instead of me, who loved her from the moment she stepped off the pod.

A breath escapes me. I have loved her from the moment she stepped off the pod, and I have loved him much longer.

"It hurts, Rihu. Smile for me, please."

His face softens, but he still does not smile. He takes a step toward me, and I want to step away, but I can't. There is only so much self-control within me, and the hug or tangle or whatever it may have been has crushed the internal protection I've been keeping around my heart. I wish to hold him. I wish for them both to hold me.

Rihu's hand comes to the side of my face and my breath halts. *What is he doing?*

Before I can stop him, his lips press against mine. It is pleasure and poison at the same time. This will taint his bond with his *ĝha*. It will taint his bond with me, and I can't allow it. Yet, I sink into him. His masculine breath tangles with my own, his hard body against mine. *Curse me,* I've needed this. My lips part with a groan, and his arm wraps around my body, pressing me closer to him.

He does not let me move as he speaks between each kiss.

"Daria does not want us to fight, *tsaĝha.* So, *do not fight me.*"

Then, our lips come together once again, and heat spirals through me. Tiny slivers of guilt and shame are still present inside me, but they're drowned out by the heat and desire I feel. It's been too long since we've been together like this. I find myself desperate for the closeness. So alone.

I don't stop him when his hands tangle in my hair, tugging at the base of my horn in the way I like most. I don't fight when he grinds against me, feeling my erection grow. Instead, I grind myself against him, making him just as hard, bringing out the heat we've both been denying for weeks. Without him, life has been painful, empty. But right now, in his arms, with his lips on mine, everything feels okay, even if Daria won't leave my mind.

Filthy fantasies of her stuck between us, feeling our cocks harden against her soft body, infiltrate my mind, dragging me from the current moment into a future I could only dream of. Not for long, though.

Rihu's hands find my waistband. While one hand palms my cock, the other works to release it from my pants. Rihu nips at my neck before whispering in my ear.

"I've been dreaming of your cock in my mouth for days, *tsaĝha.*"

His thumb brushes over the head lightly, bringing a gasp to my lips. My hips push forward without conscious thought, and I bite my lip to stifle my groan. His fist tightens, and the feel of his rough palm, his firm grip, is almost enough to push me over the edge. Rihu said he had been dreaming of my cock for days, but my mind had been worse. I couldn't sleep without thinking of him on his knees for me, pulsing inside me, or simply whispering all the things he wanted to do to me as he teased my dick like he was currently. Rihu was always better with his words.

Pulling my shirt over my head, Rihu draws a trail down my body. A hot kiss lands on my pec, then another at the center of my chest. A lick and a nip on my stomach, and then he's on his knees, looking up at me. I feel his tail wrap around my ankle, gently gliding across the skin and drawing my attention downward.

His hands skate over my bare thighs, and his eyes go wide with lust. My fingers wrap around one of his horns as I stare down at him. I can feel my heart beating in my chest, almost begging the other to begin in the same tune. I don't get a moment to feel the loneliness before his mouth envelops the head of my cock.

A groan builds in my throat as his cheeks hollow, building the pressure around my dick. My eyes close, and I tilt my head back with pleasure.

"So good," I moan, feeling him bob on my cock. His tongue flicks along my shaft as he holds the base of my cock, grinding against my *b'atu*. He works me better than he's ever done before, bringing me close to the precipice, close to begging for release. I tug on his horns, pulling him away, hoping to return the favor. He doesn't let me take control. Instead, he takes my cock down his throat, moaning around my shaft as if he's still giving me instructions.

I'm certain it's fantasy when I hear his words in my mind, but it still brings me over the edge.

"Let me taste you on my tongue, tsaĝha. Come for me, and then I'll let you touch my cock."

My vision goes blank as my pleasure erupts. As he swallows my load, my jisa shudders, and my whole body clenches. My mind shatters as I try to process what has just happened. There was a reason I was pushing him away, but it broke with the rest of my resolve as I lowered myself to my knees for my own taste of him.

Rihu always preferred to give pleasure than receive. He would often get closer to the edge by edging me than anything I could do to initiate. So, it came as no surprise when his cock gushed precome at the stroke of my tongue. It was salty and masculine, and I wanted more. He did, too.

"That's right, *tsaĝha*. Taste my cock."

Using my fist and mouth in tandem, I sucked him off as he kept his eyes on mine. The tender look on his face made my heartbeat stutter in my chest, but I didn't want to stop. Focusing on bringing him pleasure, I focused on all his favorite moves.

When I took him into my throat, his gravelly whisper nearly perked up my spent cock again. "Curse me. You're so good at that, Royi. Swallow my cock."

His whispers of approval, his encouragement, were like a haze of Helleboralis spores. Pleasure, heat, joy moved through me. I felt special to him again, just the way I desired. Then, he finished, and it differed from before. I realized where we were, what just happened, and those broken thoughts pieced back together. My overactive mind rushed to fill in the blanks. *Why was he here? Is this what he had wanted from me? What about Daria? How would she feel about what we had just done? Why would he call me* tsaĝha? *What did this mean? Why didn't my second heart beat?*

With hazy eyes and his clothes still a mess, Rihu whispered, "I've missed you, Royi."

I had missed him too, but that didn't mean he suddenly didn't have *ĝha* marks and a beautiful, perfect woman waiting for him. It didn't mean we could have clandestine meetings like this one. It didn't change a thing. Without Baso Sheva's intervention, it never would.

As if Rihu could hear my thoughts, he spoke again. "I'm helping Daria fix the pod. Then, she plans to return to Earth. She plans to leave me, and I don't know how to stop her. Not without you."

My heart felt like it was breaking in my chest, and then the sun crested the floating island land, and all my convoluted feelings fled. I was late for training. I had to go.

Chapter Twenty-Two
Royi

There's shouting at the training grounds as I arrive, and my *jisa* shudders with warning. Rihu is mere steps behind me, wanting to continue a conversation about us I'd rather not attend. Stuck between him and the scene upon arrival has me stuck in place.

Demi's legs are wrapped around another trainee's waist, her fist slamming over his head again and again as his *jisa* shudders. He drops to the ground beneath her, but she does not stop.

"Leave," I watch in horror as she changes from her fist to her elbow, striking with each statement, "Me. The fuck. Alone." His *jisa* collapses entirely, and I expect her to stop, but she doesn't. Her elbow slams toward his newly unprotected head before I unfreeze. My hand wraps around her wrist to stop her from doing irreparable damage. She's so possessed by her rage that she tugs for her hand. I tighten my grip.

"Demi. Stop."

Her eyes flash up to mine, flicking to Rihu beside me. My brows pinch together, confusion swirling inside of me about why Demi would do something like this. The other trainee warriors are her team. Doesn't she know that? When I look back at Rihu, he's beaming. He tilts his horns in approval as he surveys the scene. When I look back at Demi, her shoulders have slumped. The fight drains from her.

She's still kneeling over him, but when I let go of her hand, she shoves herself off his body. The boy she attacked wasn't bleeding, but his eye color was blown wide, and his *jisa* knit together tightly across the spot she'd been hitting.

Demi looks at the other trainees, regret clear on her face when they step back. Even D'azho. I pull her away from the altercation.

"Take care of him," I tell Rihu before stomping across the yard with my mentee. Demi had the workings of a perfect warrior. She was fast, dedicated to her craft, and, barring this outburst, the most level-headed of the trainees.

"Tell me why," I demand, tugging Demi around to face me.

"I'm not telling you shit."

Defiance radiates through her. She crosses her arms over her chest, drawing my attention to the broken skin at her knuckles. She glares in my direction, and I meet that glare with one of my own.

"Tell me," I shout.

She doesn't balk at me or shy away. Her lip curls with anger, and as I think she'll crack, she reaches for her practice blade instead. She steps into a sparring space as Rihu catches up with us.

"Demi," I warn. Her mind remains frenetic, frenzied after the fight. She should not be wielding a weapon. Stepping into her space, I swipe out for it, but she dodges. The flat side of her blade taps the outside of my leg.

"Point."

"Demi," I hold my hand out for the blade. The young warrior and I need to talk. We've gone far too long, letting our frustrations fester between one another. If my morning with Rihu left me with any truths, the one I needed would be that our adult contentions were hurting Demi. Those damned tears prick behind her eyes, and Rihu makes a sound of distress.

Her eyes slide between us before she drops her blade. It wasn't purposeful. She dropped it like it became too heavy to hold. Tears drip from her face, and she brushes them away angrily. Her tears turn to sobs, and she makes this odd hiccupping noise as she tries to catch her breath. There's nothing I can do but watch. Our little warrior breaks in front of me, and I can't help her.

I hear Rihu shift. He kneels down to Demi's level, keeping his tone calm. "What's wrong, Demi?"

Rihu is always calm in difficult situations. He knows how to move through danger and strife like it's not potentially the downfall of us all. Nothing bothers him—not me being outside his bond, not Daria's desire to leave our planet, and not the outburst of Demi. Like gusts of air, they blow right over him.

Demi scoffs but keeps her words to herself.

To help, I whisper, "You can tell us."

So many emotions shudder over her face that I can't keep track. I've learned them over the months of training with her, flirting with her sister, and helping the human women, but they all happen so fast that I miss the point entirely. Her anger returns, and she snaps, "Are you two really going to send her away? Send *me* away?"

My heart folds into itself until the edges sharpen into pain. Is this why she hurt the boy? Is this why she's crying?

I look at Rihu, but his eyes are wide. His horns tilt to the left like he's just as confused.

Before we can recover, Demi swipes up her blade and leaves the training ground.

In sync, we call out for her. Even to my ears, it sounds pitiful.

105

Chapter Twenty-Three
Rihu

"That could have gone better," I state, considering the benefits and downsides of following a grouchy teenager. Benefit, I would not have to finish hearing Royi's earlier rejection. Downside, I would have to spend quality time with a tiny girl who has no interest in my time. Benefit: I could ensure she made her way to Daria and maybe see my precious *ĝha*. Downside, I would no longer be with a person who loved me, whether or not he would admit such. Benefit—no, there were no more benefits to following the angry little girl. There were plenty of negatives, like she may still be feeling violent, or her sister could find me annoying her and decide she no longer wishes to spend time with me, or the men of the village could catch me being torn down by a much smaller foe. That would be embarrassing.

"True," Royi says, confirming my earlier fear that our conversation was not over. He simply didn't want to have it here.

"I will not wait all day for you to reject me once again," I tell him, looking to the group of gathering Vukusugo beginning their mind-stilling techniques. According to Kano and Royi, I could benefit from more peace of mind, but my mind has never felt less cluttered. A mere sliver of the sun ago, I had the best mind-stilling exercise performed on me.

"There is no future for us, Rihu."

I should not shudder with pleasure at my name on his lips, but he always had a way of making it sound like his own form of poetry.

"There is plenty of future. You will be the only thing for me after I help my *ĝha* leave me."

"Demi is right. You are dull of mind if you would let your *ĝha* leave you." He scoffs, turning toward the rack of weapons. My hand falls over his, stopping him from picking up a training weapon.

"I believe we have already had this discussion, *tsaĝha*. She would not love me if I did not give her everything I could. And you have not stilled your mind."

His eyes narrow at me, but he steps away from the weapon. Making his way to a quiet prayer mat, he kneels, and wicked images of our time on the floating island whisper through my mind. My desire for him grew stronger, surpassing my longing for anything else. Above all, I yearned for him to be in my bed, to share the mornings again, as we used to, going through our daily rituals together. I would build her a home, fill it with family for the two of us. My mother would love her as much as I did. I could promise as much. Royi would love her as much.

Kneeling on the mat beside him, I say, "If you want to have the discussion here, we can. But I will not leave you until I know we are on good terms once again."

"Good terms would require no harm to happen between the two of us."

"I am doing no harm."

"Your mere existence is harmful."

I place my hand over my heart, letting his words slide off my *jisa*. He did not mean it to be hurtful; I can tell by the way it feels in my chest. My two hearts are beating just as strong, just as healthy as before.

"If you are concerned about Daria feeling some kind of way about us, then you should speak with her. You will find she loves you as much as she loves me."

He peeks over at me from his prayer mat, annoyance clear by the scrunch of his shoulders.

"That cannot be truth."

I don't know how to make him understand what I've learned from my time with Daria and all our sweet conversations as we worked. More than me, it appeared she wanted Royi and me to be on good terms. She seemed to care for him and how our new relationship affected him, and she seemed to miss the moments when the two of us were together.

"Daria would surprise you, but you must make the first move. She would not feel right making it herself."

I'm not sure why I know these things about her. They are simply feelings inside my chest, but my words feel true as I say them. Like some invisible force, the Baso Sheva, maybe, is confirming the link between us.

"No."

"Try it for me, and if I am wrong, I will not bother you again," I offer. It was a high-risk offer, but it would be worth it in the end. I knew it in my hearts. In fact, I would bet on my second heart that it would work out for the best.

I watch him vacillate back and forth with my words. I can see his mind turning them over, searching them for any hint of malice or impending harm. So cautious, my *tsaĝha*. The urge to kiss him is an ache in my chest, but I only tangle my horns with his.

"Just try it, Royi. This is not a trick, I promise."

Chapter Twenty-Four
Royi

Bothering Daria after a long day when I know all she wants to do is see her ĝha and fix that Sheva Cursed pod isn't exactly what I would call a good idea. Yet, I find myself drawn to the idea. I find myself drawn to Rihu's *ĝha*, and I cannot tell if it is because he loves her, or because I love her, or because there is something bigger at work. Regardless of what unnatural force pushes us further together, I know that some kind of ending will come from it. As much as that ending scares me, I plow toward it.

I'm taken by the sight of her, as always. She's standing at the entrance of the *peholoe* loft, trying to decide whether she wants to enter. Her eyes slide past the large, open building and off the island's edge to the green slash across the sky, delineating the approach of night. The change in color remains lovely across her deep brown skin. The pink edges of her hair draw my attention, as well as the slump in her shoulders. She tugs at her rumpled top and sighs.

She is tired. I should not bother her.

But Rihu's promise ricochets through my mind. He will leave me alone if Daria does not want me around. If I try to be with her, be her friend, be more like he is, and it blows up in my face, then I will not have to deal with either of them. Standing tall, tilting back my horns, I approach her as casually as I can manage while feeling anything but.

She must hear me approach because she says, "You know, on my home planet, the night sky is more like the color of my hair. It's pink, purple, and blue. It reminds me of cotton candy. This just makes me think of sickness and blood."

She turns to face me, and she does not look surprised or put off to see it is me. Instead, she greets me with a smile and wraps her arms around my center.

My arms come around her naturally, but my breathing becomes shallow. My heart beats faster, the same way it does with Rihu, and I try to ignore its runaway beat.

"I haven't seen you in so long, Royi," she murmurs, her voice muffled against my shirt. That same slimy feeling of guilt slinks across my skin.

"We have been busy," I offer. It's not entirely true. I have been avoiding her and Rihu. It was too painful to see them together.

Daria peers up at me, confirming her disbelief in me, but she says nothing. She does not call me out for it or push me away. She rests her head right below my chest once again and hums her contentment. As I peer down at the woman in my arms, I wish to know what she thinks about. Is she truly this happy to see me? I have held her for quite a long time for someone who my mind said did not care about me and did not have space for me in her heart.

After another long minute, she finally steps away from me. Turning back toward the view beyond the *peholoe* loft, she stares at the sky with a long-suffering sigh.

"How long will you go before I see you again? You're making me jealous of Demi because she hears your voice every day." Daria glances over her shoulder, giving me a look I cannot decipher. Her words warm my chest.

"Maybe it does not have to be as long. Perhaps we can spend the day together tomorrow. Rihu would cover for me since I have stolen his work for many of the last days."

She raises a single brow at me. "All day? You and me?"

"Only if you so desire, Lovely Daria."

A small smile tilts her full lips, and my heart aches in my chest.

I watch her consider my words, playing them over in her mind, and I wait impatiently. Perhaps Rihu was wrong. He often was about matters of the heart. He didn't pay enough attention, and though I adored him for it, it was silly for me to assume he knew what he spoke of. From a look in her direction, I could see her mind working the same way mine was, but before she could reject me, a call came from the *peholoe* loft.

The fiery redhead, Az-ton, must have seen us and heard our conversation because she shouts, "Just say yes, Daria! Jeez."

Both of us spin to look at her, but a smile cracks Daria's face and then mine joins hers.

"Let's spend the day together. I could use a break from the escape pod, and Demi could use a break from training."

My smile grows, and I can feel my *jisa* crackling. "Great. I will arrange it."

She nods. "I know you will. Sunrise then?"

I tilt my horns in agreement. "See you at sunrise, Lovely Daria."

Chapter Twenty-Five
Daria

I think about canceling my day with Royi for about a hundred reasons. One, I'm exhausted from getting up with Demi last night. Compassion for my sister, waking up with her first period on an alien planet after blood-soaked nightmares, becomes overridden by the fuzzy sort of exhaustion in my mind. There were bags under my eyes because after Demi drifted back off to sleep, it took me hours to join her. Two, because of Demi's nightmares, she may have needed Royi more than me. Her routine was important. Three, Rihu, my *ĝha*. According to the magic sky goddess of this planet, he was my man. I was unsure if they would brand me as the newest Shojo whore if they discovered me having a good time with Royi. Simultaneously, I wasn't sure I cared since I didn't intend to stay. No matter how much Vera expected me to.

Ultimately, I decided not to cancel. Despite my numerous reasons, I get ready and check on Demi. She assures me she plans to rot in bed for the day and "mind-still." Hoga assures me she will look after her. Then, I'm out the door with a nervous stomach and a tender string of excitement to see him.

My steps are slow as I pick my way down the ramp toward the entry. He said he would meet me there at sunrise, but I'm still half-expecting him not to be there. Maybe Rihu will stand there, angry instead. Or maybe I will get stood up, even on an alien planet. My worries were for naught.

"You look as stunning as the morning light, Daria," He greets me.

"You don't look so bad yourself," I reply, feeling the warmth on my cheeks.

It's honestly ridiculous how my heart flutters at his arrival. He's dressed as he usually is, a plain shirt and tight pants that won't create more drag in flight.

"Let's get down to the flight landing."

I nod my agreement and feel like a twitterpated teenager when he takes my hand in his, leading me to his mount. The morning air is crisp, a reminder that they really have seasons here. Storm season is what they call it, though I don't plan to be around for it.

"Demi told me of your impressive feat saving Zhu's *ĝha*, Cerridwen. She says you were incredible. That you have always been a skilled *nurse*."

My heart warms at his words. Not only because he used the human term for my healing knowledge but also because there is no way Demi said all those nice things about me. Not sure who else would have told him about it. So I nod along. It's not like he and Rihu have been talking. Maybe? Hope blooms inside me.

"Are you and Rihu..." I trail off, unable to call them friends or twins or even pose the question swirling around in my head. I know the marks on my chest mean something about their relationship that it shouldn't, but I can't handle blaming myself. So, instead, I wait to hear what he has to say about them. The crackle along his *jisa,* like a scatter of electricity across the sky, tells me something I don't understand.

"He told me you missed me. Urged me to spend this time with you."

"He did?"

"Yes, he does not like the natural order of things it appears."

"The natural order?"

"*Ĝhajo*, the marks. How I am not a part of them."

My feet pull us to a stop, and he looks down at me in the dim morning light. The ugly green will cut its way across the sky soon, but I try not to think about it and long for home. I try not to wish for my vibrant hair dyes, and my polycule, and a magical fix for the pod that sits mere feet away, waiting for Rihu's mechanical hands. I try to stay present with him and hurt with him about how left out he must feel.

"You know, if the marks won't pick you, maybe Rihu and I can just decide for them."

My mind takes this opportunity to remind me I'm being silly. I'm not staying on this planet, and one string or attachment was more than enough. Yet, my aching heart screams for me to lean in, to bring him back to Rihu, to keep him for myself. To start a new relationship here in Shojo.

"That is not how the marks work, Lovely Daria. Though I appreciate the offer."

I let the conversation slide. Royi offers me his hand again, and I take it, waffling my tiny hand in his much larger one. His palm is so big only the tippy tops of my fingers can wrap around it. He slows his pace so we can walk together. When we reach the landing pad, his mount waits for us.

I greet her with fervor, whispering sweet nothings to her and practicing a few of the pre-flight whistles. As usual, Royi's mount is well-behaved. Lari waits patiently as Royi slides her harness onto her body, and she doesn't even puff out her chest as he tightens it down. Then, she bends low so we can get on. I stand with my arms outstretched, and Royi lifts me with ease.

I wrap the straps around my thighs, but Royi knocks my hands away with his. His fingers are warm as they brush across my upper thighs to pull the strap tight. The latch comes together, and he reaches across my lap for the other one. My mind wanders to his hands, and what they might look like spreading my thighs instead of strapping them into the flight harness.

I could imagine his smooth green skin pressed against mine, complimentary to my dark brown. Those long fingers would caress ever closer, careful and slow in their approach. I could see him thinking about all the ways he wanted to touch me, how slowly he would take it as he learned about my clit, and exactly how I liked it to be touched.

With hooded eyes, I glanced down at him, and his gaze narrowed in my direction. I watched his *jisa* ripple before his hands slowly dragged down to my knee and off my leg like it burned him.

Royi climbs up behind me, and his heat at my back is like a soothing blanket. His opposite, Rihu, was a man of many words, while Royi was all about physical touch. They shared a love of service, and that reminder sent a ripple of pleasure through my body. They could serve me any time. Or rather, I would serve myself up to them on a silver platter if they would have me.

I try to press my thighs together to ease the ache, but it refuses to go away. I blame the lack of sleep for my wild daydreams, but when I glance back at Royi, his eyes are stoically ahead. With a click of his tongue, Lari drops us off the edge of the floating island.

That blissful moment of freefall has my heart dropping in my chest. Then, her wings spring out, and we glide in the air.

"Shit." The feeling of the wind in my hair is incredible and wrong all at once. As much as I love the experience, I remember how long it took to detangle my curls after my first flight. With Demi's help and the oils I'd found to help the process, it took nearly an hour just to brush and detangle it.

"What is wrong, Lovely?" Royi's deep voice sends a vibration down my spine.

I have to twist my body to speak directly into his ear. The rush of the air always made talking on the mounts a little more difficult. "My hair. I forgot my cover. It will get tangled. It already is, probably."

"Allow me to help you untangle it. I have longed to feel its beautiful texture," He responds before leaning back to whistle out another order to Lari.

I did not know where he was taking us on this flight, but I trusted him. He had never given me a reason not to, even if we had talked only a little recently. I could count on Royi to be respectful of my time and boundaries. Like when I told him he couldn't touch my hair before, he respected that, even though he was now admitting he longed to feel it. My stomach does a little flop that has nothing to do with Lari's momentary dip.

"It could take a while. Demi always complains," I explain, hoping he might understand what he's signing up for.

"I am patient and gentle."

I didn't really need the assurance from him, but I appreciated it. We were silent for the rest of the ride while my heart beat like a horse at a full gallop. *Thuh-dump. Thuh-dump. Thuh-dump.* If it had been Rihu, he would have teased me for its noticeable noise, but it was Royi. He didn't say a thing, even when it didn't calm down, as he helped me from Lari's back.

We were on a part of the island that was new to me. The view from the ledge showed me the field of the beautiful purple flowers I loved as they stretched forward to the edges of the island. The sun began its ascent into the sky, and soon, the purple flowers would match that light lilac sky.

Royi allowed me all the time I needed to stare at the view before escorting me to the true destination. It was one thing I preferred about him compared to Rihu. When Royi said he was patient, it was honest. He wasn't quick to anger; he always thought before he spoke, and he never rushed me into anything. Rihu wasn't impatient, but he lacked the same ability to wait. He was much quicker to get excited, angry, or emotional in any kind of capacity. Rihu almost never thought before he spoke. Instead, he crafted wild stories within his sentences, making them come out much more poetic than he ever intended, and he often rushed me into a response—or goaded me into them if I wasn't quick enough. When my wit matched his, it always pleased him, while Royi preferred my silence as I thought out my more meaningful answers.

Conversations with the two of them together were my favorite. I had to be sharp. They volleyed off of one another so easily that, to stay in the conversation, I had to be ready for anything: their flirting, their banter, their questions. After they left, I often reeled, thinking about everything we had just talked about and what it all meant. Royi expected the most honest of answers, and Rihu expected them in a timely quip. It worked my brain like the hospital did, and until this moment, I didn't realize this was something I needed. It was exciting, and it kept me present.

"This is it," Royi announces as if it's not the most beautiful thing I've ever seen.

A colorful woven blanket is laid out on the ground next to a tiny spring of burbling water. I didn't realize there was water on this island because it doesn't pour off the side like it does on the islands attached to the karst. The water here was much quieter and calmer. It almost appeared still.

Beautiful magenta flowers the size of a quarter sprouted along the ground in a pattern similar to morning glory, but their bright blue centers made them surreal. The entire area seemed to smell like them, mild and aromatic, almost like caramel.

On our little picnic blanket, Royi had put together some of my favorite foods. It was the sweetest gesture, and also perfect timing. I forgot breakfast in my tangle of nerves. I had been too busy worrying about Demi, the date, and how I looked that I missed the urges of my stomach. They weren't silent anymore.

Royi was a perfect gentleman. He helped me settle on the blanket before finding a seat next to me. He fixed me a bowl of my own, and then he sat back and joined me as I ate. Our conversation was peaceful, and the many silences felt peaceful, not awkward. It was nice to sit and enjoy the environment with him. Even if it wasn't Earth, I could appreciate the sweet smells, the cool breeze, and the unusual sounds surrounding me. With Royi, I felt safe. Nothing could get me here, not with him around.

After our picnic, we sat and talked for a while.

"You know these flowers are used to make dyes for clothes," Royi explains, picking one of the colorful blooms. He rubs the petal between his fingertips, and I watch the color smear like bright paint. He flicks away the pulp of the crushed petal, leaving behind a bright pink stain. My smile widens slightly.

The color between his fingertips is a near match to the color my hair was when I first landed. Maybe a little darker. And the possibility of touching up my roots has me grabbing for the vine of them.

Royi smiles up at me as I pluck a handful of the flowers gently. Even pulling them from the vine stains my fingers, but I don't care. He knows what he's done.

"This is why you brought me here?"

"Among other reasons," He replies, tugging me into his lap for a kiss.

When his lips press against mine, I forget about our troubles. Time passes, life goes on, and the planet spins, but none of it matters. My desire to go back to Earth melts away with the guilt I feel for surviving out here while my dad and partners think the worst. There is only Royi, and his hands are brushing over my sides. The pressure of his lips on mine, his tongue flicking over my bottom lip. The purity of the entire moment... I know I'm right where I should be.

When the kiss ends, the feeling doesn't. Even as we stroll back leisurely to the mount, even as the wind ruffles my hair, even when we return to our normal responsibilities, I feel it. If I could have Rihu and Royi together most of the time, alone occasionally, maybe I could imagine staying. Dates like this, but with all three of us? The thought was almost enough to convince me of Shojo as my home.

Chapter Twenty-Six
Rihu

During my perimeter check, odd scraping tracks appeared beside the peholoe loft, but upon further investigation, I found all was well. Out of practice, since Royi did my work for me for days on end, I figured I missed his neurotic ways. Now that I completed my task, it was time for me to engage with the pod again.

Picking up some tools, I head in that direction.

"Rihu," Kano calls, tapping his horn against mine. Still, deep in *ĝhajo* bliss, my Rogeshu glowed with happiness. He constantly wore a smile on his lips, and his *jisa* was stronger than most. "How are you, friend?"

"I am deeply blessed and joyful," I tell him, giving him a smile of my own. Kano did not always enjoy my flowery words, but this time, he did not debate.

"It is the feeling of a *ĝha*." He said instead, practically skipping alongside me. "There is nothing better in the entirety of Shojo. Where is your *ĝha* anyhow?"

"She is with Royi this morning. I owed him many mornings of coverage with the perimeter checks."

Kano seems surprised by my admission, but he says nothing as we walk together. That is when I realized I had not seen him on the floating island for quite some time.

"What brings you to the sky warriors' domain?"

"Am I not a sky warrior and your leader?" Kano puffs out his chest before shaking himself out. That was out of character for him, and I can see his nerves. I'm attuned to nerves, thanks to my *tsaĝha*.

"Of course you are. I simply have not seen this interest since a beautiful human woman descended from a space pod."

"Well, yes. I guess I must come out with it. Can we sit?" He nods to a comfortable patch of undergrowth and we both take a seat, facing one another.

"What is happening to you?"

"My *ĝha* and I are troubled by yours. Why does she wish to leave our planet? What if it would put us at risk with the monsters they encountered before?"

I understand this fear. Before Daria asked me to help her with the pod, Royi's concerns about it were long and large. My faith in Baso Sheva confirmed all would be well, but I did not have the words to soothe Royi like I do not have the words to soothe Kano now.

"I believe she will be safe."

"I do, too. The Baso Sheva says as much, but my *ĝha* is not so easily comforted."

His *ĝha*, Vera, is a busybody. At least that's what my *ĝha* says. I'm unsure why she's so upset by it because all bodies in a village should be busy. It's a mark of good health.

We sit in silence for a moment. Kano surely working his mind to find a solution for his *ĝha*, me thinking about my own *ĝha* and how much I miss her already. I wonder if she and Royi have rekindled their own loving banter or if they will return and I will lose them both.

"Maybe you should go with your *ĝha*," Kano muses.

The thought had never crossed my mind. Yet, "I am a sky warrior, not a star warrior."

121

"We have never needed a star warrior before now, but with the rebirth of Baso Sheva, things are bound to be different."

Kano picks at the grass beneath him, mindlessly looking off in the distance. I can see his mind is riddled only with thoughts of his *ĝha*, and I can't imagine being so concerned with my own.

Daria can take care of herself. She did not need me to speak on her behalf or fight the stars. My lovely *ĝha* likely didn't even want me to. She wouldn't want that of Royi, either. Daria needed me for other reasons: to soothe her when her responsibilities became too much to bear. She needed me to listen to what she had to say and understand her weird human customs. She needed Royi, too, to understand her concerns and give her more structure here. Would she need us among the stars?

My words burst forth without merit, but I never was good at keeping my thoughts to myself.

"My *ĝha* would not want me to defend her among the stars. She would not need me if she had her family and Earth partners."

If Kano is surprised by my words, he does not say such. Instead, his voice is deep and calming when he assures me that *ĝhajo* always need each other, and if it feels otherwise, then it is because the bond is incomplete. Then, he assured me that Baso Sheva would conspire for my greatest good— which I already knew. My trust in Baso Sheva never wavered. In her death, she spared my mother. In her rebirth, she brought me Daria. If only she would bring me Royi. The future could really begin.

Chapter Twenty-Seven
Daria

I'm not ready to be done with Royi, and he doesn't seem finished with me either. After we land and care for Lari, his hand caresses the side of my face. He glances at the *peholoe* loft beyond, and then his eyes trail my face.

"Shall we detangle your hair, Lovely Daria?"

I glance at the *peholoe* loft and think about bringing Royi to bed. I want to march him straight through the loft and to my bedroom. All my wild thoughts course through my mind at once. His muscular hands in my hair, his scent all around me, this mild itch beneath my skin being scratched for good. I want that experience for myself. Not for all the *peholoe.*

"Yes, but not there."

We stop by anyway and grab the things we will need. A wooden pick comb, the specialty oil Hoga gave us, and the special-smelling soap I loved. It was a cross between lavender and eucalyptus. Then we walk through the village together. I want to hold his hand, and I want to flirt with him. Yet, he focuses on our surroundings, safely guiding me toward the hot pool hidden in the tall purple flowers. It takes an entire sliver of the sun to get there by foot, but we talk the entire time.

"What do you find most difficult about our planet?" Royi asks.

In all the conversations I've had with Vera, with Hoga, with Demi, no one has asked. They've assumed it was all about getting home to my partners or my dad. They guess it's because I loved my job and my life. Maybe they assumed taking care of Demi on my own was some big hard task, but no one ever asked. Not even myself.

"Wupeso is beautiful. There are so many stunning things about this island that don't exist on Earth. I'm grateful I'm able to help, that I'm not here alone, that I have this opportunity to be literal Lightyears from my home, but I'm exhausted.

"Every day I wake up with the sun, trudge up and down what feels like a billion uneven steps, help women who are happy and fulfilled in this world, keep track of Demi who doesn't make it easy, rinse and repeat.

"On Earth, it wasn't like that. Exhaustion was temporary. Each day was different. I had this massive support system built into my life. I want that back. It's like I hate this planet because I never have the bandwidth to enjoy it."

I swallow back the heavy words on my tongue. Was I focusing on the wrong things? Going home was nearly impossible. Was I wasting extra time and resources when I could refill my energy by leaving behind something I couldn't reach?

"What about today? Are you exhausted today?"

"Yes. Exhausted but happy."

My companion smiles, and I slip my hand into his. His eye color widens quickly before returning to normal, and he gently squeezes my hand. We continue our walk, meandering around as we chat.

Royi always asks the best questions. From asking about my partners on Earth, which feels like a big step, to asking what my favorite thing about Shojo is, we chat about the differences in our cultures. He explains more about him and Rihu growing up together, and how long he's loved him. He calls Rihu his *tsaĝha,* and when I ask him what that means, he tells me it means he chose Rihu to make his second heart beat, and even if it never did, he would always treat him like he did.

"But he's been so alone since the marks showed up," I said. It wasn't a question, but he answered me anyway.

"I have been trying to respect you. It is not fair of me to love him the way I do when he is bound to you. In fact, it's sinful."

"Never thought I'd be the old ball and chain," I grumbled, feeling even worse for tearing them apart. So what if Baso Sheva decided I was for Rihu? He and Royi had been inseparable until me. I ruined something special, and for what? When people on Earth called me greedy for wanting more love in my life, it never bothered me, but the word came unbidden to my mind now. Did my greed for love taint their goddess's view of me? Did she have to show me the error of my ways?

No. That was the nonsense of my upbringing that I had done the work to undo. I simply loved Rihu and Royi together, and their love for each other was one thing that drew me to them.

"A bond is not a burden like this ball-and-chain saying suggests," Royi explains as we enter the field of lavender-colored stalks. The steam from the pool beyond thickens the scent in the air like a diffuser until the calming floral reaches my nose.

"I certainly feel like a burden. Like I'm the reason you and Rihu aren't the same anymore."

Royi's long-suffering sigh is a direct representation of how I feel inside. His hands come to the sides of my face, tilting my chin up to look into his beautiful green eyes. His face is so serious I can't help but melt beneath his words.

"Lovely, beautiful, Daria. Never, ever think that *you* are a burden to Rihu and me. We simply weren't ready for the shift in dynamic. That is as much my fault as it is his."

"So, you and Rihu, you will get back together. You still love him?" I ask, feeling my heart stomp a wild beat in my chest.

"I could never stop loving him, could never let him go. Even for a woman as beautiful and capable as you."

My mouth feels dry as I ask, "What if I didn't ask you to? What if it could be the three of us?"

Inside, I'm asking myself the same questions. *What if I didn't ask him to give Rihu up? What if it could be all three of us together? Would I want to stay here then?*

"That would be the dream."

I push myself toward him, resting my hands on his chest for support. He meets me halfway, and then his lips crash to mine. The world seems to swirl around us. The smell in the air falls away until all I can smell is his masculine scent. All I can feel is his shimmering *jisa* beneath my palms and his lips on mine.

He kisses how he speaks, thoughtful and direct. He doesn't waste time with a teasing preamble but rather dives into exactly what he wants, asking for entry with a swipe of his tongue. My lips part for him, defaulting to his command.

In his arms, I feel my need for control slip away. It's like I could trust him to care for me and take care of my concerns while Rihu made life more fun. We come away from the kiss, gasping for breath, and a sharp pain in my chest makes me hiss.

Pulling my top away from my skin, I see my marks flaring to life across my skin. They feel raw, and when I look back at Royi, I see amazement written across his face. Pulling off his shirt, he reveals pecs I want to kiss and two stunning marks across each.

"What does that mean?" I whisper, my fingers skimming over the marks. It couldn't be what I hoped. The lavender-colored stalks dance behind him, and I draw my eyes upward.

Rihu steps into the clearing behind us with a bright smile on his face and announces, "It means we're all *ĝhajo*. We're *b'ijàchinĕ* like the goddess."

Chapter Twenty-Eight
Daria

B'ijàchině, the word Hoga said weeks ago, curls through my mind as I look at the two beaming men in front of me. I understand now. *B'ijàchině,* as in some alien form of polyamory, available to me, blessed by some unknown goddess. And it's all right in front of me. Love, devotion, and balance between the three of wait.

Demi steps out from the stalks behind Rihu. Her brown eyes, deeper than mine, glare.

"Rihu fixed the pod."

I'm mated to two stunning alien men, but a mere hour away on foot stands an escape pod that can take me away from it all, back to normal. It can take me back to Earth with much better odds than before and return me to Anthony, Malik, and Nasha. Back to cocoa butter massages, electricity, long Greenbelt date night walks, and board games full of bickering. Back to my dad, who I miss almost as much as he likely misses us, and the hospital that I couldn't step into after my mom died.

"Are we going back?" Demi asks, stepping in front of Rihu and Royi.

It's all I've wanted. Since we landed, I pleaded for anyone to care about the lives we left behind. I wanted my dad to know I was alive, for my partners to rest easy. Returning to them was my only goal, but now...

"...I don't know, Demi. Probably."

She scoffs, turning on her heel to disappear back into the trees. The sky seems to jump above us, its loud *boom* reverberating through the ground.

"Go to the loft," I shout in her direction. I'm not sure I heard her perfectly, but it sounded like she shouted back, "Go to hell!"

My shoulders slump. What am I supposed to do now? Two alien men bound to me here, my family left on Earth; I felt stuck.

Rihu and Royi study me with wide color in their eyes, my hair products forgotten on the ground. My vision goes blurry, but I don't realize I'm crying until a salty tear drops to the ground, and a thunderous clap cracks in the sky above me.

"Daria, what if you stayed?" Vera's words start. Then, all my memories flood my head at once.

First, it's one of my mom and dad, the night I sat them down to tell them about my romantic situation. I was so nervous my hands were shaking. I didn't know if they would understand. Or if my love for them was contingent on a traditional marriage and life. But, we sat down, and I told them about my partners and my mom said, "Are they cute? Do you have pictures?" My dad's only concern was if Anthony liked football, since Malik wasn't the biggest fan.

After all was said and done, and I was heading home for the night, my mom pulled me aside. With my dad cleaning up in the kitchen, it was just the two of us on the porch. A cool autumn breeze stirred through my hair, ruffling my mom's silk bandana. She eased the door closed behind her and pulled me into a hug. With her lips practically against my forehead, she murmured, "Your heart has always been big enough for a hundred people. I'm glad you finally realized it."

Next, there was the time our little polycule rented a cabin in Colorado for Christmas. The main suite had a huge Alaskan king bed, decked out with flannel throw pillows and a stuffed bear the hosts named Snuggles. We were all laid flat, staring up at the mirror on the ceiling, wondering how that design choice fit into the woodsy theme.

We were all a little high, and Nasha was well into the esoteric part of her bliss. She was humming lightly, making the rest of us sleepy, then she sat up abruptly and scared us all half to death. We thought she forgot a lit joint downstairs or maybe a family member's birthday, but she said, "If I die young before we can all get married, I want you all to throw a wake for me."

It sparked an entire conversation about whether we would reincarnate and fall in love again, and ultimately led to us all talking about our dream funerals. Anthony wanted a band for his funeral march, Malik wanted streamers and a catered luncheon because he said funerals were such an inconvenience, and when they turned to me and asked what I wanted, I told them the truth. "I just want our plots stacked together, one right beside the other." They thought it was cute, but I realized now that if I didn't go back to Earth, that would never be the case. They might put my name on a headstone, but my body would be billions of Lightyears away. Maybe they already had.

Unfortunately, that wasn't even the worst memory to assault me. It was the third one that made me emotional enough to open the skies above me. The rain started as I remembered everyone sending us off to space.

The launch facility was like nothing any of us had ever seen. Beyond the militaristic gates, there was a cutting-edge facility with floor-to-ceiling, rocket-proof windows and bustling families all around. We, as in my polycule and my family, both made a road trip to the actual launch, and it was finally time to board the shuttle that would take us to the moon. While my dad said goodbye to Demi, reminding her again and again that she had to be good for me, I was saying goodbye to my partners.

"Ladies first," Malik had teased, pushing Nasha in my direction. She was nothing like the confident girl I had fallen in love with at that moment. Instead, she seemed nervous. Her brows pinched together, and she struggled to gather her thoughts. She kissed me like it would be our last and then said nothing before passing me off to Anthony. I found it odd at the time, but now I saw it with fresh eyes. Afterward, I said my goodbyes to Malik and Anthony. I gave my dad a hug, and he promised me he would be okay, that by the time we returned, he would be okay again. Better. We were walking away when Nasha called, "It's okay to move on, D. We will always love you." I thought nothing of it then, but now…

The sky seemed to let loose. Fat drops of stinging cold water poured from the sky, cascading over my skin painfully. Then, Rihu and Royi were there, crouching over me to block out the worst of it. I was already soaked through, and my teeth were chattering. Looking ahead, I could barely see through the deluge, but it didn't matter. Rihu's warm hand met my back, and then Royi's came to meet it on the other side. Their fingers brushed, and sparks seemed to ignite inside me.

"The empty hut behind Kano is closest," Royi says, turning to look at Rihu. He tilts his horns in agreement, knocking them against Royi's before they push me down the trail. Their legs are much longer than mine and they set a punishing pace until my legs are shaking and I'm slipping on the water-logged path.

I can feel panic growing in my chest. Is Demi safe? Did she make it back to the *peholoe* loft? How can they tell where we're going? Surely, we've passed cover by now? What if we walk right off the cliff? Hot breath pulls me out of my reverie.

"How can you look this good, half-drowned by the storm?" Rihu whispers. A new rush works through my veins, and the chill of the storm melts away.

"She must be designed beautiful," Royi agrees, his hand creeping just a half-inch lower.

"If she looks this beautiful like this, can you imagine how stunning she would be on her knees for you?"

My following gasp had very little to do with the icy rain and more to do with the heated bodies behind me, protecting me from the storm. The snap of thunder in the sky didn't even break the bubble of warmth they'd built for me.

My eyes flick to Royi, and I can see his assessing look. At this moment, he's more like me, unsure of the return of their banter. Then his mouth curves up, and my insides melt.

"All I can imagine is how good she'd look taking your cock at the same time."

I want to press my thighs together to ease the sudden ache, but the pressure of their hands on my back keeps me at pace, unable to pause for an even breath. Rihu's eyes seem to shine as they draw me even further down the path. The rain hasn't let up, icy winds and thunder roar, and yet, under their crouched protection, I'm melting. I want to take off my warm, wet clothes and feel their hard bodies against mine.

"Almost there, Lovely," Royi says, pointing out a foggy light nearby.

"Then we can get you out of those wet clothes," Rihu adds.

As I glance between them, I wonder if galaxies away would be far enough to escape what's coming. Then, I wonder if I even want to escape.

Chapter Twenty-Nine
Rihu

Together, we led her right past the light and into the smaller hut right behind Kano's house. It was a perfect place to get out of the storm. Kano kept it stocked with extra village supplies, like food and glow crystals, and linens, and it was warm since the earth beneath it ran on the heat of the springs we had just run from. I only hoped he wouldn't freak out about us ruining his organization system, as we were bound to do.

 Once we were all inside, Royi immediately stripped off his clothes and laid out a half-dozen extra blankets. He made quick work of the space, turning it from a storage space to a cozy room to wait out the weather.

Regardless of our best attempts to block the worst of the storm, Daria's teeth clicked together in a worrisome rhythm, and her body shook as she tried to untie the strings of her top. The cold soak of the storm in my clothes bothered me much less than watching her suffer, so I finished stripping out of my shirt before brushing her hands out of the way and untying the knot at her neck. She shivers beneath my fingers, and I can't help but smirk.

"Nervous?" I ask, leaning my chest closer to her body to help her warm. Her usually warm lips were leached of color.

"Abow-about wha-t-t-t?" She chatters, leaning against me with a pleasurable groan.

Her body is almost as cold as the rain crashing down from the skies outside, but I don't mind when she presses it against me. Royi joins us in the doorway, a fresh blanket in his hands. Daria drops her top, baring herself to him, and I watch him harden at the sight. If it weren't for my own icy pants, I would be right there with him. Hell, seeing him grow hard for our *ĝha* tested my blood even with the soaked garment clinging to me. Her fine behind brushes against me as she slips out of her own chilled pants, and the fire inside me wins out. My cock is as solid as the hull of her fixed pod.

Daria steps out of her pants, and Royi wraps her in the blanket, covering the broad expanses of soft, brown skin and wrapping her in his arms. He has linen wrapped around his waist, and he's holding another out for me as I finally finish stripping out of my wet clothes. Before I wrap it around my body, I shake my head to get rid of all the excess droplets and run the linen over my hair.

Both my *ĝhajo* stared at me, open-mouthed with awe. I love their bodies just the same, but it feels good to see the approval hidden in their bodies. Royi's hand flexes against Daria's shoulder while her eyelashes flutter low. The tiny dots of her vision trained on my cock. The way they look at me almost makes me want to leave the linen off, but then a draft whips through the hut, and tiny bumps rise on Daria's skin, and I remember keeping her warm is more important than thinking with my dick.

I wrap the linen around myself, bending to kiss both of them. First, Daria—a tiny brush of my lips across the center of her forehead, which I've learned from the other women doesn't hold a third eye. Then, Royi—a tangle of horns and a press of my lips against his. I can feel her between us, her warm breath on my chest, and it makes me smile against Royi's lips. Between the two of them, I could find myself quite busy keeping their minds quiet.

"Better?" Royi asks, his eyes scoring across me like a blade on a grinder.

"Warmer," I agree. Royi spins Daria into my arms before turning back to our clothes. He pulls them all from the floor, wringing them out into a pot, and hangs them out to dry.

When he's finished, we move toward the mound of blankets and tuck Daria's voluptuous body into the makeshift nest. It looked more like a pile of laundry than a bed, but as the storm raged on outside, we agreed it would have to work. Her teeth kept their cacophonous clatter even as we piled in beside her, trying to drown her in our heat.

Royi's hands brush across her skin gently, and I watch the odd bumps return. His voice is soft when he whispers, "You know, you would be much warmer with a *jisa*. It protects us from the sun, but also the elements."

"Yes, well. There's only so much I can do about that." She pouts, turning her back to Royi and snuggling into my side. It's an obvious snub, but one I cannot allow. Now that we were all bound, I could do what was best for us all rather than just what was best for my *ĝha*. With one hand beneath Daria's head, I reach for Royi, urging him to come closer, but I can feel his hurt within me. He tangles our hands together and comes to rest against Daria's back.

"We're all bound," Royi starts.

"Which means your *jisa* waits for one thing." I finish, tilting her face toward mine.

Our lips meet in a soft caress, and I feel Royi's hand leave my own to brush down her side. We've never shared a partner between the two of us, but I'm confident we can bring her into this moment with us with ease. She's stunning, and Royi and I work well together. We have a rhythm that we've shared for years, and she is the harmony we've been waiting for.

Dragging her leg over my hip, I create space for Royi to move to touch her soft center. Then, I pull away, ignoring her protest as I rest the base of my horns against hers.

"Do you want us, Daria? Do you want us to part those lovely thighs and take you? Make you ours?"

I watch Royi's fingers skate across her skin, dipping between her legs and to the glistening folds there. As they brush through her curls, her body tenses, and a sensual hum curves in the air.

"Tell him," Royi demands in her ear, his eyes locked on mine. His hand rubs circles right above her center at the tiny dot of pleasure there.

"God, yes. Don't stop. Please."

A smirk tilts my lips. "I love to hear you beg," I murmur against her skin, working ardent kisses down her body.

Together, Royi and I lay Daria on her back, trying to keep as much of the covers on her *jisa*-less skin as possible while still making her hot with our touch. As her hooded eyes turn to meet his, Royi steals a kiss, and my shaft hardens further. The two of them look so incredibly right together, and it's a wonder I ever existed without the two of them in the same room like this.

Daria reaches for me with one hand, tugging me back down to them, and I join her. With my lips and teeth, I nip and suck her delicate skin, feeling its softness against my tongue. Her sweet sounds feel the air, half-drowned by the storm raging outside us.

Gratitude for this moment warms my chest, scattering across my *jisa* and making my hearts feel so full I think I need a third. The two *ĝhajo* in front of me are my everything. One, old to my heart, like a worn heirloom. The other is fresh, like the year's harvest. Both were fulfilling to my soul as if their light belonged there the entire time. To see them like this, vulnerable and open to me, trusting me, is almost more than I can take.

When my lips graze the skin right above her curls, her soft exhalation reaches my ears. Royi's ministrations move further down. His fingers curl into her pussy, and my tongue brushes over the luscious skin of her cunt, circling her clit. Together, we work our newest partner into a symphony of moans and pleas, focusing on bringing her to the peak of pleasure.

"Fuck, that's good," Daria says, her hand circling my horn as her thighs tremble. Her scent is intoxicating, her taste invading my senses. Tangy, sweet, *mine*. I work my tongue over her, wishing for more of that scent and flavor on my skin.

We feel the moment right before we push her over the edge. Her body tenses, her hands tighten on my horns, pressing me tighter against her clit, as I suck the tiny bud into my mouth, flicking my tongue over it. Royi's groan of pleasure, as he murmurs, "So tight," reaches my ears, even as her thighs press in around them. Then she screams with pleasure, her voice fighting to beat the storm outside with the one we've created.

Royi removes his fingers slowly, and I lap at her wetness as her pleasure ebbs and the sensitivity takes over. Daria's sounds of pleasure turn to soft hums and then a giggle as she glances between the two of us.

"That was out of this world."

Royi and I look at one another. If the skies beyond our world contained pleasure like that, we would be more than happy to bring her home.

Chapter Thirty
Royi

The pleasure was good at erasing her plan to leave from my mind. With my fingers drenched in her scent, her taste, I push them into Rihu's waiting mouth, feeling his shiver of pleasure and the soft pressure of his tongue against the pads of my fingers. His face glistens from the way she came so hard on his face, and I tug him forward to get a taste of her on his tongue. My cock was hard, insistent with need, as I got my first taste of Daria on Rihu's tongue.

The guttural groan of my old partner tangles with the soft mewl of my new partner as she watches the passionate kiss we exchange.

"Are you ready for us?" Rihu asks her, bringing her half-lidded eyes to meet his. Her words tumble out in an unintelligible jumble, and Rihu's signature smirk grows. He looks at me, his smirk turning to a smile as he says, "It is as the humans say; we have *scrambled* her mind."

My heart tells me to tease, offering to unscramble it with her through another incredible orgasm, but my fear speaks louder. It tells me to keep her mind scrambled because if I do not fix her sexual haze, maybe she will stay. My selfish thoughts are enough to make me soften slightly, so I keep the teasing nature instead. I fall back into the routine with my partner, the flirting with Daria.

"Maybe we can unscramble it."

Daria stretches out her body with a sweet smile. "And how would you plan to do that?"

Rihu captures her nipple in his mouth, giving it a rough suck as I palm my cock. Her tight cunt would clench around it tighter than Rihu's fist. I imagine sinking into her wet center, feeling her pussy flutter around me when she came, like she did on my fingers. *Curse me.* I've never been so hard.

Rihu curls his arm around her, putting his wide palm at the center of her back. And it's like I can feel it myself. He urges her to her knees, placing her on the pile of bedding with her back curved seductively. He kisses her roughly, and her nails scrape through his light hair like mine have a hundred times before.

"Open your mouth for me while Royi claims your pussy, Lovely," Rihu demands.

I'm not sure if this will work, if the sexual encounter will provide her a *jisa,* or if there are more partners for the three of us she must meet before it covers her skin, but I know that these acts of intimacy bring on the protective barrier for the humans. It was the case with Vera, according to Kano, and Priscille, according to the pirate. But they were not my *ĝhajo* nor my responsibility. The Lovely Daria is. If we take this step, and it can protect her, I want it. Even if it cannot protect her, I want it. I ache for her. Now, we must make her want this so we can deepen our bond further and protect her.

Daria consents to Rihu's words, her mouth dropping open to him, sticking out her pink tongue for his cock to glide across. Rihu guides the head of his dick into her delightful mouth, and she moans around him. I want to tell her I feel the same way, that he tastes as good as she does, and that I wouldn't mind cleaning her pleasure off of his dick, but I don't.

Instead, Rihu tilts his horns to me, ordering me around in his special way. "Enter her with me, *tsaĝha.*"

With my cock notched at the entrance of her swollen pussy, I run my hand down the center of her back, watching it curve under my touch. Gripping her hip in my hand, I whisper, "Are you ready, lovely?"

She nods, bringing Rihu's cock further into her mouth, and I press forward slowly and smoothly, giving her little time to adjust.

"*Curse me*. I can feel her moaning around my cock." Rihu grunts.

"You're taking me so well," I say, bringing my hands to her hips. "You're taking *us* so well."

Her garbled moans of assent, and the squeeze of her walls around my cock, are nearly enough to send me over the edge.

Chapter Thirty-One
Daria

My blissfully blank mind tries to understand the words spoken above me.

"You're taking *us* so well," Royi praises as he slides his cock out of me once again. He's so big that I can feel every inch and curve as he pulls out halfway before thrusting into me once again. Meanwhile, I try to focus on the cock in my mouth and Rihu's hands on the edges of my hair, still respecting my boundary even though it's a mess from the flight and the storm, and feeling the tension of his fist would be a welcome sensation.

Rihu hits the back of my throat, and I remind myself to breathe through my nose when I gag. Tears prick my eyes, but I don't mind. Flicking my tongue along his length, I moan at his distinct taste on my tongue. His gentle hands at my hairline, guiding me up and down his shaft while he joins in on Royi's praise, feel right. The feel of both of them inside me feels right.

"I bet her cunt feels better than flying. Just like her mouth," Rihu says, still guiding my head as Royi increases his pace from behind. I hollow my cheeks, sucking him harder. "Just like that, Daria. Doesn't Royi's cock feel good?"

My pussy clenches at his dirty words. Royi groans.

"And what about Rihu? I love the taste of his hard cock."

Images of Royi on his knees, sucking Rihu's cock, flutter through my mind like the memories of Earth did earlier today. I can see him on his knees by the edge of a bed, fisting his own cock as Rihu shuttles into his mouth with abandon. I watch him rub Rihu's pelvis with a free hand, pulling the masculine sounds I want to hear from Rihu's lips. Then I see an image of Rihu returning the favor, taunting Royi to come on his tongue. I can feel my pleasure rising, the heat coiling in my belly, the feeling of fullness from Royi's cock. My moans grow uncontrollable as they work together to slide me back and forth between them.

As Rihu's cock hits the back of my throat, Royi pulls out halfway. When he slams in, filling me to the brink, Rihu pulls out until just the tip of his big cock rests on my tongue. Back and forth they go, working in tandem with their bodies and their words. They praise, caress, and thrust into me like two halves of the same whole. The weeks of discord between them are long forgotten as they work together to bring me to my second orgasm of the night.

I feel it build inside me. The heat curls, my muscles flutter, the tension builds, and then they thrust into me together, speaking in tandem.

"Come for me." They demand, grinding into my holes and bringing me straight over the edge with me. I feel their cocks swell inside me, and I come so hard I see the stars in my vision as waves and waves of pleasure rock over me. I have no idea how long it lasts, but they pull out of me gently, helping me back under the covers, whispering sweet nothings in my ears until my eyes flutter shut and exhaustion takes me into the pleasant darkness of sleep.

Chapter Thirty-Two
Daria

I wake to the feeling of pins and needles on one of my legs. As my eyes adjust, I see why. Rihu slung his heavy leg over mine while Royi cuddled half-underneath me, pinning my leg between them. They begin to stir with me as I wiggle my dead leg out of its prison.

The sounds of the storm have faded, and through a tiny window, the sky appears slightly lighter outside the storage hut we found ourselves in, but the ugly green-gray clouds still populate the sky in fluffy pockets of impending rain. Yet, the worst of it seems gone and everything that happened before comes rushing back.

The pod is fixed. Demi ran off again. *Did she get out of the storm?*

"Wake up," I order the guys, shaking them both gently. My clothes are still damp, but I don't care. I pull them on anyway, expecting their chill against my skin. When it didn't come, I looked down to see if maybe they were drier than I expected, but I found a sparkling membranous *jisa* instead. Centered on the green marks at my chest and radiating out is a light silvery-sage shield that acts like a second skin.

Medically, I'm entranced. Fear fills every other crack inside me. I don't *feel* any different, and gliding my hands along my skin is better than before. Aside from the extra shine, I truly can't tell what the *jisa* does from looking alone. If I didn't have Blossom's scans and bloodwork on the datapad and Roxie's illness as proof of what happens when you ignore your *ĝha* (*ĝhajo* in my case), I wouldn't be panicking. Since I was the most educated on the topic, aside from the AI, breathing became difficult.

"What is this?" I ask, pointing at my skin. The guys look at my skin, tilt their heads toward the marks on my chest, and skim their wide eyes over my body with pleasure, making me squirm.

"Looks like your *jisa,*" Royi said. At the same time, Rihu gives a more flirty answer.

"Looks like my *ĝha.*"

I glare in their direction. "You two are no help. Clean this up, and meet me at the *peholoe* loft. Got to make sure Demi is safe."

I don't wait for them to get their act together. Stomping out the front door of the hut, I tuck my head down and walk back to the trail, not expecting to run smack dab into, "Vera! Sorry."

"Daria? Sorry. That was my fault. I wasn't looking where I was going. I swore the hut was this way, but I guess I'm still a little turned around from the storm."

"No, you're on the right track. I hunkered down there to wait it out."

We stand there in awkward silence for a minute, and then I hear the guys stumble out together, already bickering. Vera looks from me to them, her mouth dropping open. Then, she recognizes the spark of my *jisa,* and I release a breath, hopeful she will say nothing. Of course, wishful thinking meant little in reality.

"You didn't," Vera gasps. Rihu and Royi come to stand half a step behind me, and like idiots, one drops a hand to my waist while the other bends to smack a kiss on the top of my head.

"This changes nothing," I retort, holding my hands out placatingly even as they shake.

"Daria," Vera says my name in a way that makes my stomach drop. Her head tilts to the side, and her eyes soften. The compassion in her gaze makes my lips tremble. I don't want to hear her next words; I don't need her to tell me this changes everything because I already knew that. Luckily, she knew that too. "Are you honestly trying to leave still? Did you even think about what I said before?"

Peeking over my shoulder, I see two alien men who adore me. The love in their eyes makes my heart clench, and my shaking hands worsen. When I look back at Vera's seeking face, I nod. I've thought about it alright. I've thought about how I would lose everyone I ever loved on Earth, throwing in the towel on escaping, and how I'd have to admit that everyone was right about me. My heart was big enough for a hundred people, and a bunch of them were here with me. Leaving would be a mistake.

A tear escapes, and I brush it away with a half-giggle.

"I'm going to stay."

"You're going to stay?" The guys ask in unison.

"She's gonna stay!" Vera announces, her smile beaming as she drags me into a hug. When she finally releases me, I see Rihu and Royi have tangled their horns together, whispering under their breath to one another.

Vera brushes her hands down her pants and straightens up. With her celebratory smile, she says, "Well, now that those storms have passed, I've got to be a Rogeshu's wife again."

"And we've got to find Demi," Royi adds as they detangle.

Excitement rushes through my veins, and I spin back toward the path. "Yes! We have to tell Demi. Oh my god, she'll be so happy."

"You haven't told Demi?" Vera calls, her blonde brows wrinkled.

But we're already rushing down the path together, joining hands as we go. Demi was going to freak.

Or maybe I was going to freak. Demi never went back to the *peholoe* loft.

"You haven't seen her?"

"No. I assumed she was with you," Hoga tells us. The weight of my *ĝhajo*'s concern settles in my chest, as if it has always been there, an inseparable part of me. I know it's not mine, Rihu's is too foreign and Royi's too practiced to be my own.

"Shit."

"Maybe she's with the young warrior, Sadie," Royi offers.

"Or at the training grounds."

I know they're trying to help, but something in my gut tells me they're wrong. Despite being bound to me, they don't have years of experience with Demi. She was furious with me during the storm; she stomped off to do what?

I close my eyes, thinking like my sister. If I were Demi, where would I go?

"The pod. She's at the pod."

The three of us move fast, my own legs making two strides for every one of my *ĝhajo's*. We bound over the bridge to the flight grounds in search of my sister, shouting her name as we go.

"Demi!" we cry out, our words overlapping like our fear. Turning into the clearing, I can see the pod. Lights are flashing all over the pod's exterior, flashing and spiraling through the trees. I hear the shearing of metal and my heart goes cold inside my chest.

"Demi!" I shout, running toward the pod. I'm stopped by my *ĝhajo,* as one of the vicious monsters from the *SS Herculean* appears in the doorway.

"Wait here," Rihu orders, stalking forward to attack the nearly impenetrable creature. It feels like my insides are trying to leap from my body, and I ignore his command, walking forward a couple of steps. There's no way I'm letting that monster get my sister.

Royi's hand lands on my shoulder, and he forces me toward the tree.

"Demi!" I scream again.

"We can't help her if you're in the fray," Royi explains, his hand brushing over my hair. His lips press against my forehead and I feel the truth of his words. I plant my feet on the ground, watching as my *ĝhajo* move forward. Royi yells, "Where are you, Demi?"

Despite her muffled voice, I'm certain she's screaming when she says, "I'm here in the pod."

My men run toward her at full speed, and I hear her yell for help. Two of the monster's legs exit the tiny pod, crushing the ramp under its weight and I force myself to stay still.

"Help her," I whisper, hearing my *ĝhajo's* response deep in my chest.

Chapter Thirty-Three
Rihu

Sheva curse me. What in Shojo is that? A monster that looks like it belongs at the bottom of the chasm crawls backwards out of the broken entry to the pod, shearing metal as it tries to escape something on the inside. No, not something. Demi. The fierce little warrior.

"Oh, fuck me," Daria curses behind us, backing up from the creature and taking a half-step behind a tree. It was quite large, but we knew this was a possibility. Kano told us about the creatures from beyond the skies. He warned us we may see them. I only wish I listened to what he said about them.

"Is this what brought you to us?" Royi asks. I wonder if Daria can hear the undercurrent of concern in his tone like I can. I wonder if she can feel it along her *jisa*.

She nods her assent, then tilts her head in our custom. Before we can come up with a game plan, a flash of light comes from the other side of the monster, and it rips a larger hole in the pod's side to escape.

A bright sac stands out on the beast's underbelly as he straightens on the ramp leading to the ground and something inside me says Kano told us about this, that it's the key to destroying this foul creature.

As it scuttles back toward us, Demi waves the light in front of the beast again, sending it another step backwards and towards us.

"Daria, you wait in those trees. Rihu and I will take down the beast and send Demi to you."

My beautiful *ĝha* backs away from us slowly, keeping her eyes on her sister at the shredded pod entry. Demi looks quite fierce, but Royi and I both knew she was a natural warrior. Brave, honest, and willing to fight for what she believes in were all qualities we looked for in our youth, and Demi had them in excess. The creature she faced was five times as big as her and could probably swallow her whole or kill her with one swipe of an armored leg. Yet, she faced him down with little more than a glow crystal and a tiny blade.

"Evil beast," she shouts, waving the light in front of it and taking another step forward. The disgusting creature roars, its dozens of eyes looking away from the light as it swipes at her with a damaged claw.

Royi is at my side in a moment, marching forward in step with me as we advance on the creature. He explains what I missed from the meeting with Kano.

"To kill the creature, we remove that bright sac beneath it."

"Easy enough."

"Do not be foolish, Rihu. We must protect Demi at the same time."

I look at the young girl before me. As the claw swipes out at her, she smacks it with the tool and stabs out with her blade, cutting through the flesh of the creature's arm. It hisses and growls, but she does not care. She bares her teeth in its direction. Though I can see the tear tracks on her face and imagine her fear, she does not appear to need our help at all, except maybe to show her where to sink her blade.

"It appears she can protect herself."

Demi lands a particularly hard hit on the beast, and its claw shatters into pieces on the ground. I catalog the weakness in hopes I never need the knowledge again.

From the treeline, I hear my beautiful *ĝha* call, "Now that's my sister!"

The beast turns away from the little warrior, turning its attentions to my *ĝha*. Protective instinct spins inside me. I can feel it like a reflective pool inside Royi. We look toward one another and advance faster. If the creature thinks it will reach our *ĝha*, it is sorely mistaken.

I lose track of Demi as a protective mist descends over my vision. To ensure my ĝha stays with me, I must slay this beast. To prove I can keep her safe. That I can keep her sister safe. I am so distracted by my fear for my *ĝhajo* that I must miss the killing blow. The little warrior must have done something extreme because the beast scuttles the last few steps down the ramp and then tumbles straight to its face in front of us.

Chapter Thirty-Four
Royi

The little warrior killed it. I kick at it with my boot and not a single one of its many eyes opens. I am stunned as the young Demi stands from her kill, holding the tool and blade in her tight grip. Daria rushes forward, past both Rihu and me, and wraps herself so tightly around the little warrior I worry for her safety once again. The tools clatter to the pod ramp and send the birds scattering from the trees.

We should celebrate her and name her a proper warrior. My mind whirs with the implications of her first kill.

"What the hell were you thinking? Why weren't you in the *peholoe* loft? Why did you come out here during a storm?" Daria asks, her voice quavering even as she shoots the questions at her sister faster than arrows from my bow.

Demi, high on her kill, hugs Daria back tightly before explaining. Her hands shake, but her words are solid, her mind is clear. I can see it in her eyes.

"I didn't want you to leave, so I came here to sabotage the pod. Then, I got here and started to breathe and practice my mind-stilling. I didn't want to destroy anything permanently from a temporary emotion." The little warrior's eyes meet mine for a moment, and I give her a tilt of encouragement. "Anyway, I was about to pull one of the electrical plugs, hoping that it would be easy to just pop back in, when all the lights went dim and the monster came. I hid behind the panel, but then it came in and started ripping stuff out."

"We believe they're intelligent." I offer before I can think it through. Daria's eyes widen, and I feel her disbelief in my chest, so I snap my mouth closed once again. Demi continues.

"I'm not sure how it started, but I hurt it, and sparks happened, and then this crystal glowed, and the creature didn't like it, and I didn't know if I was going to live, so I just attacked. I kept pushing him back, trying to beat him, hoping you guys would find me soon. And then," she huffs a breath, as if she can't quite believe it herself, "And then I killed it."

A nervous laugh bubbles out of her as she stares at the corpse of the creature beneath us.

"I wasn't even sure that was going to work," she laughs again.

"What?" Daria half yells, crushing her sister in another hug. Her reprimands come with no heat, only relief. "You psycho."

"This is an impressive kill," Rihu admits, looking at the creature. I am with him. I want to pull it apart myself and see what we can learn about it, but now is not the time.

"Don't encourage her," Daria squeaks, looking Demi over for any major bleeding. The girl has a couple of burns and bruises, but nothing a warrior couldn't heal from in time. I watch her fingers shake and turn to find her some water.

Truthfully, I didn't know how humans would react to the high of their first kill, nor one so honorable as this, but it appeared the little warrior was buzzing. Not an inch of her body didn't wiggle as she laughed and hugged her sister. Grabbing my cup from the work table, I fill it with some of the fresh rainwater and bring it to Demi.

"You should drink."

Daria helps her, stabilizing her hands as she drinks. Droplets of water fall from the cup and onto her soaked clothes, but Demi barely notices. Her eyes dash from corner to corner, taking in her kill and the surrounding forest. Now that the storm has passed, the last slivers of the sun shine on the lands again, and that light filters through the trees.

Rihu has made his way into the pod, and when he pops his head back out, he announces, "It appears the pod may need some more repair."

Demi's head snaps toward the pod. Her eyes are frantic as she searches the hull, her eyes falling to the cords upon the floor. The crunch of the ramp, and divots in the walls. Her happiness falls rapidly as she looks at the disaster and back to Daria.

"I'm sorry. I'm so, so sorry. If I hadn't been in there, maybe the beast wouldn't have ruined it. I swear I wasn't going to do anything. I was just thinking about it. I had decided against it. I swear."

Daria runs a soothing hand over her head, pulling Demi into her chest once again. For the first time since the kill, the little warrior seems truly concerned. She did not wish to hurt her sister. She only wished to stay.

"Demi. Demi, listen," Daria commands, tilting her sister's face toward hers. "We're going to stay."

Demi's smile falls completely. The salty tears I've grown used to from the little warrior fall. She tries to shake her head, but Daria holds her steady, nodding in the way humans do.

"We're staying?" Her voice cracks, and the events of the last few minutes finally take her over.

Striding forward, I pick up the small girl before she crumples. Daria places her hand on my arm, looking down at her sister with a soft smile.

"We're staying, Sis."

"But what about dad? And Anthony and Nasha and Malik?"

"What about Royi? And Rihu? And Hoga?" Daria replies. Demi curls into me, sobbing into my chest. I can never tell what the emotion is behind her tears, but I believe that is the point. There is emotion. Maybe I do not need to understand it.

"So we're staying? Really?"

"We're staying," my *ĝha* confirms, and I feel her honesty in my chest.

Together, all four of us walk back to the *peholoe* loft, where I set her down. Daria helps the little warrior wash and dress before checking her eyes with a small light and calling for Blossom to do the same. When my *ĝha* is content with her sister's comfort and health, she slips out of the room to meet with Rihu and me.

We've been waiting rather impatiently. Or rather, I have been waiting in silence while my *tsaĝha* spoke nonstop about how wild the beast was and how incredible of a kill the little warrior made. His frenetic pacing would annoy most, as proven by Hoga's narrowed eyes and her open palm across the base of his horns. But to me, it was endearing. It was the Rihu I knew.

"She is experiencing a little shock, but Blossom says we don't need to worry about her vitals."

"You are certain?" I ask, hoping Demi's mind will stay strong throughout the event.

"She said as much," Rihu answers for her. He uses some of his extra energy to kiss our *ĝha*, and when I open my mouth to ask more questions, he plants his lips on mine, too.

Chapter Thirty-Five
Daria

One Moon Later

"Remember when you wanted to leave?" Vera asks, sipping *tsare* with her feet up. All the women are here, even Roxie. And all the women are annoying me, especially Roxie.

"I remember what it was like trying to resist," she says with a groan. "My arm itches just thinking about it."

"You hardly resisted," Aston rebuts. Going on almost a year of resisting her alien, she would be the expert on that. Plus, I didn't resist my guys. Once our marks showed up, my sound plan fell apart in less than three months.

"Not everyone can be President of The Mate Hate Club," Roxie spits back, setting down her own glass of *tsare*. One she told us all she shouldn't even be drinking.

Priscille's belly is huge as she waddles in. Demi slides a stool over for her and offers an arm to help her sit. The ex-nun gives Demi a kind smile and leans on her a little harder than I would have expected. Demi doesn't even falter under the pregnant woman's weight, though. All her warrior training strengthens her with each passing day.

"Arguing isn't good for Priscille's baby," I tell them all, effectively shutting them up.

"Fine, we won't argue about who has been the silliest about their mates. Which isn't me, for the record," Vera announces.

"No, of course not, you could do no wrong," Comes Aston's sarcastic reply.

To avoid the two of them bickering senselessly, I turn to face the room in my gown for the first time. The fabric is silky like Vera's was, but instead of a light blue, it's a stunning magenta like the edges of my hair. The light of the glowing crystals in the room catches the material, making it appear like I'm wearing some kind of liquid rather than the gown itself. Both Rihu and Royi made me a wood bangle for my upper arms, and they're decorated with stunning emeralds to complement their skin. That's right; my men made me jewelry so I could look better beside them. Ridiculous.

The women catch sight of me and gasp. Demi spent all day yesterday braiding cornrows in my hair and creating a beautiful bun at the back. Then, this morning, she helped me with my makeup, mixing all her shades on my face to make me feel better than I ever did in makeup on Earth.

"They're going to shit their pants when they see you," Roxie says, making the rest of the women burst out in laughter.

"You look stunning," Vera agrees tactfully.

"Do you think this is crazy?" I ask Demi, ignoring the responses behind me. Vera snorts, Roxie gives a tentative 'well,' and Priscille says, "Of course not."

"This feels a little crazy," Demi replies, checking to ensure I'm flawless from head to toe. "But no more crazy than me killing a monster, or the pod dropping us here, or going to space on your mom's dying wish."

I give her a nod. She's right. Of course, she's right. I should have been listening to her the whole time because she had adjusted. While I was busy freaking out about a way to get home, burying myself in work for the tribe, and wondering if I was ever going to make it home, Demi was acclimating. She was taking the punches that were thrown her way and setting herself apart. She was giving herself a purpose and begging me to see it.

I pull her into a hug, trying to keep my tears at bay. "I'm so glad you're here."

Her arms wrap around me tentatively. She whispers back, "I wouldn't miss this day for the world."

Before I know what's happening, Priscille is sobbing into my ear and wrapping her arms around me tight. Roxie and Vera are there too, and even Hoga joins in on this huge group hug.

My heart was big enough for them all.

Chapter Thirty-Six
Royi

"I don't understand why we can't see our *ĝha* yet. I miss her beautiful eyes and her fingers digging into my shoulders while I—"

"Rihu, stop," I demand, trying to fix my ceremonial clothes. They're entirely too fine for me, and that Rihu must wear them also is absurd. He can barely keep his flight clothes clean on duty, let alone ceremonial clothes for an entire evening.

"Don't you miss her?" He whines.

"Of course I do, but she's getting ready with the women. It's bad luck to see her before the *r̈uṣad'ù*."

He scoffs. "You just don't love her as much as I do."

The glare I toss over my shoulder shuts him up, but he still whines.

"I just want to see her. Those warm eyes, that smooth skin, the way she responds to us when she likes our kind words."

Before I can respond, Kano joins us in the room of Jaye's house. She left ahead of us slivers ago to prepare the fields for the ceremony.

"Tisugo," He greets, straightening his own ceremonial robes. They differ from ours since he is our Rogeshu, but he looks just as uncomfortable as we do.

"Rogeshu," we respond in unison.

"Are you prepared for your *r̈uṣad'ù*?"

We both tilt our heads in agreement as I finish fussing with my clothes. I prepare a blindfold, tying it around my wrist to offer it to Pa when we reach the caves. A metal band wraps around my fourth finger. A human custom that Daria wanted us to ascribe to since she would not have had the opportunity on Earth.

"Well, I am here to escort you, then."

"Finally," Rihu exclaims, tapping his horns against Kano's. I fall into step with them outside Jaye's home, and Rihu twines his tail with mine. My nerves soothe slightly but even more when I see the crystal fields before us.

Before the women arrived, neither Rihu nor I were much for praying. Kano was our devoted leader. He prayed enough for the three of us, we believed. Then I saw Daria exit the pod with the women. I learned her name from the sunthetic intelligence woman, Blossom. I learned she was a healer on Earth, and I wanted her from that moment forward. Daria's smiles, her laughs, even her sadness. If only I could fix it. To me, it didn't matter how long it took. I simply knew she would be perfect for me, perfect for Rihu, and perfect for the three of us together. I hate that I ever held doubts.

At the entrance of the cave, Pa removes my blindfold from my wrist, tying it around my eyes until my vision is gone. He does the same with Rihu by my side and leads us into the darkness of the caves.

Together, our hearts beat in sync. I can feel his steadiness as if it's my own, thumping to the same steady rhythm while we await our *ĝha*. Then, we are told to open our third eye, and the energies of the crystal field fill our vision while the thoughts of our *ĝha* fill our heads.

Chapter Thirty-Seven
Rihu

It is not enough to hear her soft voice in my mind. I need to see her; I need to see her aura in the vision of my third eye. Being back in the caves, to bind with Daria as Royi and I did early in our adulthood, reminds me of that time. I hope to meet Daria with the same ferocity I found Royi.

Then, our marks did not show, but neither of us cared. We entered the caves under the cover of dark. We took our places, bound our eyes, and opened to the magic of the caves. Together, we fought the phantom spirits of ancestors and met each other near the exit. Seeing him through my third eye for the first time left a crack in my chest that I waited for Baso Sheva to fill. One that he soothed for years and years until the women arrived.

Now, my hearts both beat in tandem, just as Royi's did beside me. I could hear them and feel their echoes in my own chest.

"*Are you two coming to get me?*" Daria asks in our minds. Her voice there seals a crack.

"*We are on our way,*" Royi answers before I can ask her if she wishes for us to, before I can put the power back in her hands.

We move through the caves and the colors blend and dance, but a single golden thread seems to weave through the space. A single thread belonging to my *ĝha*.

Royi must see it too, because his pace improves. Though, if I remember right, finding our *ĝhajo* was never the troublesome part. Royi and I were drawn together like waves upon the shore. He could be without me no longer than I could him. This was no different. Our hearts wanted to see her, touch her, be with her.

"Are you walking toward us, Lovely Daria?" I tease within our mind bond. To feel her presence there, the patience and love she holds for us, the excitement for our future, would bring a lesser *Vòllø* to his knees.

Her steps echo through the cavernous walls, creating a tune. Our steps like the pounding beats, hers like the harmony to our song. A complete moment just waiting to happen. Her acquiescence resonates in my mind and reverberates throughout the chamber. Then she's standing in front of us.

Royi and I move in tandem as if our bond truly strengthened us to be one and the same. We secure our hands around her wrists, bringing her closer to our bodies. Her scent fills my lungs, and everything feels right again.

"I'm never spending a morning without you again." It's my declaration and my vow.

"And I vow to protect you always," Royi adds.

"I swear to tell you of your beauty forever until you look upon me with those shy eyes that I love."

"And I vow to bring smiles to your face."

"From this moment forward, you're a piece of me, and I will keep it with me always," I finish, pointing to my wedding ring.

"I vow to wear the symbol of your love," Royi says for his third. Daria, her eyes hidden by her own blindfold, smiles in our direction.

"My vow," She begins, pausing as if she can feel me leaning in, pleading for her words to leave her delectable lips, "Is that I will stay with you until the end, where we will be placed together until whatever life might come afterward."

We each take our turns kissing her, sealing our vows before Baso Sheva rather than the people of the village, as Daria requested. Then we exit the caves.

Chapter Thirty-Eight
Daria

My blindfold remains when their voices whisper in my mind that we've exited the caves. Rihu removes my blindfold for me, his stunning green eyes meeting mine before he places a kiss on my forehead. I can feel Royi's hand on my back, and the village cheers for our arrival. Yet, the *r̈ uṣad'ù* doesn't feel done.

"Weren't we supposed to face something in the caves? Some kind of challenge?" I ask.

"Maybe the monster during the storm was enough," Rihu offers.

"Your choice to stay here must be enough, lovely *ĝha*," Royi assures me instead.

Yet, it does not feel quite sealed. Then, Priscille cries out, and the crowd turns toward her. The sand beneath her feet now clumps together, soaked and dark, as her eyes meet mine through the crowd.

"I think the baby's coming."

I throw myself into action. Directing my guys, my *ĝhajo*, to help her back to her home, the village follows us. I time her contractions as the parade of people celebrates. Another human-*Vòllø* child and another successful *r̈ uṣad'ù* all in one night was a blessing unlike any other.

Six hours later, Priscille and Mekho welcomed the healthy baby Estelle into Shojo, and when I held her in my arms, I could hear my mother's voice. *Touch the stars, Daria. Hold them tight.*

Epilogue
Aston

"I swear to God, Aston, you're stronger than this," I say, pointing a finger at my reflection. My girls are dropping like flies to the drug that is having a *ĝha*. First, it was Vera, happy to jump Kano at first notice. Then, it was Roxie, literally going to a different island to follow her *ĝha*. Now, even Priscille has jumped the single ship–literally. Most recently, my staunchest warrior fell because, and I quote, "Who can resist two?" As president of the Mate-Hate Club, I can't fall, no matter how badly I want to. There are women counting on me. Yet, my feet carry me out of the *peholoe* loft silently, under cover of dark.

Alien dick isn't even that good, I tell myself as I make my way down the steps of the karst. That I've made it this far proves I'm lying to myself, but I still try to justify my behavior. I could always go to Vera's instead. It wasn't like I had to go to Llazho's place. It wasn't like he was expecting me like he would be disappointed if I didn't show. The lies pour through my mind like the sweetest honey, begging me to take a taste.

I could already see him in my mind, leaning against his doorframe, waiting for me. He always looked so handsome, having ditched his shirt the moment he got home. His *ĝhajo* marks glow in anticipation of my arrival. Then I saw the creased brow he would get when I didn't come around the corner, the downward turn of his lips while he waited and waited. I could imagine the sag of his head, the way his tail would go limp. I could imagine the slight paling of his sea-green skin.

As my feet moved, I knew I needed to stop this. I shouldn't keep leading him on like this when I could never be a proper partner. I shouldn't keep indulging in him just because of my own selfish needs. My behavior was selfish. I knew this and yet couldn't stop myself from doing it, anyway.

I finally pulled myself to a stop before the last turn to his home. Even the location of his place was perfect. He lived right above the sandy drop that led to the cove's beach. It meant he could roll out of bed each morning, step out the door, and practically be at work, and it meant I could fall asleep in his arms to the gentle sloshing of waves. It meant that when I got a silly idea in my head to meet him on the beach one night and have my first non-alcoholic sex on the beach, he indulged me and then brought me straight home afterward to clean up, so the sand didn't burrow in terrible places. He cared for me and caressed me, telling me all the reasons he would love me forever.

Yet, for me, it wasn't too late to turn back. I could go back to the floating island and sit there until the sun rose, telling stories like Roxie was still here. Slip right past him, and head to Vera's, find a place against Magnus and fall asleep for the night. I would probably even be welcome at Priscille's, as long as my waking her up didn't disrupt her sweet darling daughter, Estelle. As I considered all my options, as I reminded myself this was getting out of hand, I somehow began moving again.

Then, I was there, and he was standing in the doorway, as I imagined, but his brow was smooth, and his face was bright. His shoulder was against the frame, and his arms were crossed in front of him, drawing all my attention to the magical tattoos on his chest and the curve of his biceps. When he saw me approach, his gaze bore into mine, and I could feel my resolve melting into a puddle. The Mate-Hate Club was the last thing on my mind when Llazho looked at me like that.

He didn't move to meet me. He never did, and I always wondered why. I wondered if he thought it would scare me off or if he wanted to give me every second to back out. I never did. No matter how much my mind pleaded with me to.

Standing in front of him, my eyes trail up the bulging muscles of his chest, meeting his piercing eyes. I reach my hand up to his face, and only then does he move. Quicker than I can comprehend, his hands wrap around my wrists, and his lips crash to mine. The guilt fades entirely, and everything feels right as he brings me inside.

Everything moves fast. It always does the first time I return to him. My legs wrap around his waist, grinding against him, his fangs nip my earlobe. I'm hot and wet, and I need him, but he knows all that. He moves us to the bed, and in no time at all, I'm stripped of my alien clothes, feeling him move inside me, grinding myself against the tiny pleasure bumps at the base of his cock.

He makes me feel so full, whole, and healed; I hate and love it in equal measure. He works me until I get close, and then he always makes the same demand.

"Look at me, Wildfire."

My eyes snap open, and I come with him. It's always with him. Even though that should be statistically impossible, it happens with him every time. His face contorts with pleasure, but his eyes never leave mine. Then, he slips out of me, and his forehead comes to rest against my own.

I don't want to let him go. I don't want it to be over, so I tuck myself in close as he rolls to the side. My thigh goes over his hip, and my head rests on his chest, and the sound of his breathing lulls me into a perfect, wonderful, nightmare-free sleep I can't achieve on my own.

In a few hours, he'll wake me up and give me the opportunity to sneak back to the *peholoe* loft. I'll feel my guilt like a cement block in my stomach, but I'll walk away. I'll see him throughout the day and give him every ounce of vitriol I can stomach. I'll spearhead the Mate-Hate Club, and make secret art of him in the abandoned apartment I found connected to the loft, and protect my secrets with all I've got because they're the only things keeping me from making the biggest mistake of my limited life.

ACKNOWLEDGEMENTS

This was my most challenging alien book yet.

So, thank you to my team. The beta babes really gave phenomenal feedback under the constraints I gave them. My husband stuck out every meltdown, and my writing buddies were there to lend an ear.

A new (and amazing) person joined the team for this project. Cassie (@cassiew012 on Fiver) acted as both a beta reader and sensitivity reader for the piece. Daria and Demi are both women of color, and Cassie helped me ensure they were represented properly. Beyond that she provided detailed and helpful direction that changed the story into what it is now. I can't thank her enough.

Finally, thank you reader. I appreciate you most of all.

BOOK CLUB DISCUSSION

1. How does the concept of fated mates impact Daria's plans and emotions? Do you think this concept adds to or complicates her situation?
2. What challenges does Daria face in her role as healer for the village?
3. What moral dilemmas does Daria face, and how does she handle them? Do you agree with her choices?
4. How does the revelation of the fated mate marks on one of the men, but not the other, affect the relationship between the two alien men? How do they navigate this unexpected twist, and what does it reveal about their bond and individual characters?
5. Which scenes had the most emotional impact on you? Why do you think they were so powerful?

Thank you for reading "Daria's Aliens"! If you've enjoyed the book and would like to stay connected, here are some ways to do so:

Visit MadisonValePublishing.com

Sign up for our mailing list to receive exclusive content, book recommendations, and notifications about new releases directly in your inbox. Stay in the loop and be among the first to know about any exciting developments.

Follow @madi.vale on Instagram

Consider leaving a review of "Daria's Aliens" on platforms such as Goodreads, Amazon, or other book review websites.